Frid...

DATE
dress

Ashley:
Seek beauty,
Spread sunshine!
Talena Winters

TALENA
WINTERS

 My Secret Wish
PUBLISHING

Published by My Secret Wish Publishing
www.mysecretwishpublishing.com
Contact the author at talena@wintersdayin.ca.

ISBN (print): 978-0-9947364-0-6
ISBN (eBook): 978-0-9947364-1-3

Cover and Title Page design by Fiona Jayde Media,
fionajaydemedia.com
Edited by Lora Doncea, editsbylora.com

Stock photos:
Woman in Red © / Shutterstock.com
Handsome Indian Man © / Shutterstock.com

Author Photo: Talena Winters

To my parents, who taught me to love stories.
To my husband, who gave me a love story.

Acknowledgements

I owe many people a debt of gratitude that this book exists.

Firstly, I want to thank my parents, who have encouraged me many times that I should be writing fiction.

Extra-special thanks go to my husband, who endured my many nights in front of the computer, listened to me bounce ideas off of him, and even read my manuscripts (although he doesn't usually read romance novels).

I am thankful to the readers of my blog, *Winters' Day In*, whose many encouraging comments to write a book helped me believe I could.

Thank you to Laurel Easton and Laverna Stanley, my VIPS (aka "beta readers.")

Thanks go out to Holly Lisle and Kristen Lamb, whose teachings and passion to help writers succeed gave me the confidence and tools I needed to take the leap.

To Lora (www.editsbylora.com), my editor and formatter—your kind and encouraging words and coaching were invaluable. Thank you for taking my book from good to great and being good-natured about the American/Canadian "language barrier."

To Fiona Jayde, thank you for making my dream cover design a reality.

And to you, my readers—thank you for reading my story. I hope you come to care for Peter and Melinda as much as I do.

CHAPTER ONE

Melinda dropped her keys and purse on the kitchen counter and closed the door of her tiny one-bedroom suite. She kicked off her work shoes and sighed in relief as her throbbing feet sunk gratefully into the hall carpet.

It had been a typical Thursday working at the diner. Truck drivers, cops, and local shop owners kept her running all day—every one of them lousy tippers. She wondered why Sandra never complained about her tips. But then, with her fluffy blond hair, doe eyes, and flirtatious smile, she could collect tips just for showing up at a guy's table.

Melinda paused to glance in the mirror by the door, then turned away. She knew what she would see—dark hair pulled back in a messy ponytail, tired grey eyes, mouth set in a firm line. It had been years since she could smile at all, much less produce one like the dazzler Sandra flashed more often than cameras at a wedding.

1

Her perpetual melancholy drove her boss, Fred, crazy.

"Myers, you gotta smile," he had snapped again that morning. "No one wants to be served by a waitress looking like she'd rather bite 'em than feed 'em."

"Sorry, Fred," she said. "I thought I *was* smiling."

"Really? Show me."

Melinda forced out a smile.

"You gotta be kidding me! Looks more like you just ate your dirty laundry! Listen, keep chasing away the customers with your attitude, you're through here, ya hear me?"

Melinda nodded, wide-eyed, scooped up an order of fish and chips from the pass-through, and fled to the dining room. Seriously? She would be fired because she wasn't Vanna White? What about her hard work and accuracy with orders? *And I have never 'chased away a customer.' I get pretty much the same people every week.*

Still smarting with the memory, she looked back into her hall mirror with its chipped lacquer frame and put on the same smile she had shown Fred earlier. He was right—there were more sincere smiles on a used car lot.

Melinda sighed in frustration and made her way to the bedroom. She skirted around the floor-to-ceiling cardboard boxes stacked high in the tiny living room. They blocked out any view of downtown Calgary, but there wasn't much to see—just someone's windows across the street. She carefully hung her gaudy blue-and-white diner uniform with its too-cute frilly apron on a peg behind the door, then threw on the same jeans and black Henley top she had already worn two nights in a row. They still smelled fresh enough, and she wasn't trying to impress anyone, anyway.

Melinda leaned on the kitchen counter and munched on a carrot stick. The microwave hummed behind her with a small Styrofoam cup of soup on its turnstile. She twisted her engagement ring while she waited, caught herself in the nervous habit, and forced her hands to stillness by planting them on the counter. She diverted her focus to the task ahead.

A half-finished dress was hanging on a linen-covered mannequin, calling to her with the allure of a mythical siren. She resisted just long enough to slurp down the soup, toss the container in the garbage, and splash water on her hands and mouth. Then she slipped around a small round table buried in sewing paraphernalia and stood in front of the dress—a vision in grey and black and pink. After a moment of caressing the edgy skulls-and-roses silk crepe, she set to work.

In the wee hours of the morning, she finally crawled into bed—exhausted, but triumphant—with the completed dress hanging from the top corner of her bedroom door. A smudged pencil sketch of the design was attached to the front, a seal declaring its

3

finished state. Before she drifted off to sleep, she gave the gown one final, satisfied glance.

Yep, Robert would love it.

"Melinda-Honey, would you take table eight? I want to go on break soon," Sandra drawled as she floated by with a tray of drinks. Melinda nodded and fished in her apron for a pen and pad as she crossed the checkered floor.

The couple at table eight was more interested in chatting than reading menus. Hearing their playful, affectionate banter, she felt the familiar twinge of pain in her chest, but suppressed it and tried to put on a brilliant smile.

She glanced at Fred, who frowned. Fortunately, the couple didn't even look up.

"Hi," she said to the tops of their heads during a break in the conversation. "Can I start you with something to drink?"

The dark-haired, mocha-skinned woman who glanced up actually made Melinda catch her breath. Women that beautiful rarely came into Fred's Diner. Okay, never. Melinda jotted down the woman's order of iced tea. She didn't need to write it down, not really—but she did need an excuse not to stare at the woman. East Indian, she thought, from both the clipped, succinct accent and the way the woman reminded her of the actress on a Bollywood movie poster she saw every day on the way to work.

The man finally looked up and doubled the iced tea order. And she dropped her pen.

If the woman's looks made her catch her breath, the man's made her forget that she knew how to breathe at all. Bottomless black eyes, black hair, perfect teeth, a dimple—it was just not fair for that much beauty to be sitting at one table. The man could have been on the Bollywood poster right next to his companion.

Melinda nodded mutely at his order, scooped up her pen from the floor, and fled back behind the counter. Her face flushed right up to her hairline.

What would Robert think of her? *Acting like a schoolgirl!* She continued to berate herself as she filled two glasses with iced tea and then popped in lemon wedges and straws. After two long, slow breaths, she headed out to the floor and barely trembled when she placed the iced teas in front of one of the most attractive couples she had ever seen. She took their meal orders and served them without further humiliating herself.

Melinda kept tabs on the couple as she served her other tables. When they had both pushed their plates aside, Melinda returned to collect them. Oddly, the man was observing her with a penetrating stare. She locked her eyes on the dishes—stacking the woman's empty plate on top of his in one hand and grabbing the empty glasses with the other.

"Refill?" she asked, not looking up.

"Yes, please." The man spoke. "And I think we'll have some of your mud pie for dessert."

"Oh, Peter. Really? I can't eat that!" The woman looked mortified and pleased at the same time.

Melinda's eyebrows lifted as she looked at the tiny woman. She could certainly afford a little pie. Then she thought of the small Styrofoam soup cup that had contained her entire meal the night before. *Like I can talk.*

"Preeti, it's not every day that we get to celebrate you landing your dream job. I'll share it with you. You can have a few bites, can't you?"

The woman hesitated.

"Chocolate. Chocolate. Chocolate," Peter chanted until she grinned and nodded.

"Okay, just a bit."

Peter turned to Melinda. "My sister is the new fashion editor at *Fresh* magazine," he said. "This is our celebration date."

Not a couple, then. Brother and sister. Melinda felt a little flush of heat creep out of her collar.

"Not every girl is lucky enough to have her brother take her to a *truck stop* for a date," Preeti teased. Then she gasped and looked up at Melinda. "No offense."

"None taken," Melinda replied, surprised to find herself with a small—but real—smile on her face. It felt so unusual that she stood there, enjoying the

6

sensation for several moments. She was still standing there smiling stupidly when Preeti spoke up.

"So … the mud pie? I guess we'll take one after all."

"Oh—sorry! Of course. I'll be right back with it." She hurried away, the heat wave overtaking her face completely.

Preeti shook her head slightly at the waitress' retreating back. "That girl is a little odd," she said in a low voice. "Too bad she doesn't take better care of herself. She could be quite attractive."

"Well, she must be doing something right. She's engaged, after all. You saw the ring, right?" Peter had glanced at the pretty waitress' left hand out of Single-Guy Reflex, and felt a twinge of disappointment to see the fourth finger encircled with a gold band sporting a sizeable diamond. He knew his older sister—who missed no attire detail on anyone—would have seen it, too. Her nod confirmed it.

A vision of his girlfriend Anise's face flashed in his mind, her fiery red hair falling in waves to her shoulders. He fidgeted with his cutlery. *Old habits die hard, I guess.*

The ponytailed waitress whisked back to their table with iced tea refills and a layered chocolate dessert on a plate with two forks. She set everything down and left without a word.

Peter grabbed his fork and then caught the expression on Preeti's face. He froze and narrowed his eyes.

Peter knew that look all too well. It was the one Preeti wore when she was about to meddle in his life—for his own good, of course. He had experienced the repercussions of her "helping" more often than he cared to remember. He opened his mouth to stop her, but she spoke quickly.

"I wonder if they have hired their wedding photographer yet," Preeti said, indicating the waitress with her fork. She shaved off a small bite of mocha ice cream and slid it into her mouth. Her eyes grew wide. "Oh, this is good," she said, nodding. "You've got to try this, Peter."

Peter gave her a look of mock exasperation for her meddling. "You can ask her, if you're so interested." He took his own mouthful of chocolate heaven.

She put up her hands in self-defence. "Hey, if you don't start making money as a photographer soon, you'll never be able to take me somewhere nicer than a diner for lunch." She slid the plate closer to her and scooped up a large portion of the dessert.

"Not all of us have hit the big time, yet, sis. But I'm working on it." He glanced out the window. "Being a delivery truck driver may not be glamorous, but it pays the bills."

"Oh, Daddy must be so proud. His son the engineer, pinching his pennies as a UPS driver."

"Stop eating my head! You know I don't want to be an engineer, any more than I want to drive that truck for the rest of my life, *diidii*." The Hindi word for "older sister" dripped with sarcasm, a reminder that they were not children in Mumbai anymore.

She flashed a dazzling smile. "You know that I'm just teasing, little brother." She scooped up another huge bite and closed her eyes in rapture.

Peter scowled and aimed his fork at the dessert, surprised that his sister had already consumed most of it. He glanced up at Preeti, who was licking off her fork with relish. She looked over at him mid-lick and he shook his head, eyebrows lifting in amusement.

"'A few bites,' my butt!" He smirked, pulling the plate out of her reach to finish the last few bites himself.

"Oo, look who is learning the local slang!" she said, and then reached out to scrape up a little more chocolate from across the table.

Peter curled his arm protectively around the plate and fended off her fork with his other hand, grinning at her tenacity.

"Never you mind," she scolded, and put her fork down.

Peter chuckled and finished the last bite during the cease-fire.

Preeti watched him relish the final bit of ice cream cake, then got back to her point.

"Seriously, Peter, you are a very talented photographer, you just need to promote yourself more. You need to get a proper portfolio put together. I want to be able to hire you at *Fresh*, but I'll need to show them something more than snapshots of our friends on Facebook to prove that you know what you're doing."

"I will get to it, Preeti. Stop eating my head!" he exclaimed again.

"When?" Preeti asked, steely eyes holding his.

Peter was saved from responding when Melinda flew up to their table on thick-soled white sneakers. She wiped her hands on her apron before speaking.

"Can I get you anything else?" she asked, eyes focused on the blue Formica tabletop.

"Yes, actually," Preeti replied, turning toward Melinda with a gracious, well-practised smile. She ducked her head toward the girl until Melinda was forced to look at her. "My brother here is a talented photographer, and I can vouch that he is quite good at what he does. He's too shy to ask, but he was wondering if you have already hired your wedding photographer."

Peter's eyes shot darts at his sister.

The girl winced. "Wedding photographer?" She started twirling the ring on her finger with her left thumb and bit her lower lip, her eyes suddenly moist. "Um, no, we haven't. My, uh, fiancé, Robert, he's a pilot. He's gone a lot, so we haven't had time to work out a lot of the details yet."

Peter couldn't make sense of her reaction, but he weighed his options. Starting his photography career with a wedding was enough to make his insides curdle, but he knew Preeti was right. There was no time like the present. If his older sister—who rarely wasted compliments—believed he could do a wedding, well then, maybe he could.

"Peter," he said, thrusting out his hand toward the waitress. She hesitated, then took it. "And this is Preeti, my sister." He nodded toward Preeti. "Uh …" he squinted at her name tag, "Melinda. May I borrow your pen?"

The girl handed it over, and he scribbled his name and phone number on a napkin. He gave it to her, and she stared at the scrawl in black ink.

"I'd love to be your photographer, if you are interested," he said, infusing as much confidence as he could into his voice. He ignored the smug look he knew would be on Preeti's face. "Give me a call, and we can get together when it works best for you. I'll show you some of my stuff."

He hesitated, chagrined at his own nerve. *What stuff? Landscapes and bumblebees?* "Well, what I've got so far, anyway. Photography isn't my full-time gig— yet—but I am … working on it. I'm usually off work by about 5:30." He jerked his thumb at the cube delivery truck visible through the window, as if the tan-and-brown uniform he was wearing weren't explanation enough. He did a mental face-palm. *Way to work the sales pitch, bro.*

"I get off then, too," Melinda said. She seemed a bit dazed as she folded the napkin and tucked it into her apron. "Uh, thanks, P-Peter. I ... I will. I'll give you a call." She dropped the bill on the table between them, gathered up their dirty dishes, and was gone from their table faster than lightning in a summer storm.

"Strange girl," Preeti said. She shrugged. "I guess it takes all kinds."

"It does. Doesn't it?" Peter aimed the comment toward his sister, who did not look the least bit embarrassed by her audacity. He shook his head. Preeti had always been that way.

As Peter sipped the last of his iced tea, he watched Melinda scurry around the diner as though on autopilot. She did her job thoroughly and efficiently but without an ounce of joy.

Maybe she was having a bad day. But he sensed not.

"I think she's lonely," he said, mostly to himself.

"Lonely?" Preeti replied, following his gaze. "She's engaged!" She paused and watched Melinda take an order from a nearby booth. Her every mannerism seemed to declare that unnecessary interaction was not welcome. "Well, maybe. I can't help wondering if that ring is some form of defence against unwanted attention. Some waitresses do that, you know. Maybe she's not engaged at all."

Peter remembered the odd look Melinda gave him when he asked about her wedding photographer, and shrugged. "Well, if her fiancé is gone as much as she says he is, she just might be lonely."

"Not our problem," Preeti said, suddenly all business. She slid out of the booth clutching a red patent-leather bag which Peter knew would have some fancy designer's logo on it. "I have to get back to work. A fashion editor's work is never done, you know," she said in a sing-song voice.

"Let me give you a lift," he said, scooping up the bill and fishing his wallet out of his back pocket as he stood up.

"Seriously? You think I want to be dropped off in *that*?" She flicked her eyes to the truck. "I'll take the bus, thanks. It's only about ten minutes to the office."

"Suit yourself." He grinned at her. "See ya later, sis."

Preeti headed for the door, and he made his way to the till to pay. He only had to wait a moment for Melinda to show up to take his money.

"Say, uh," he began, not quite sure where he was going next. She glanced up, then back down at the keys, pecking furiously. "Hey, my girlfriend and I are going to the movies tonight … you know that theatre down on Macleod Trail?"

The waitress nodded, and the cash register jingled.

"Eighteen ninety-five, please," she said.

He handed her a twenty and kept talking. "Maybe you … I mean, you and Robert, if he's around … uh, would you guys like to come on a double date with us? And if he's not, you are still welcome to come. Anise is really great. She won't mind at all." He hoped he was right about Anise not minding. Things hadn't been going so well between them lately. Women could be funny about having other pretty women around, he'd noticed, even if they were on the arm of another guy.

And the girl looking at him with those wide, grey eyes was definitely pretty, just a little … tired, maybe.

She cleared her throat as she handed him the change. "Uh, thank you, but Robert is flying in this afternoon, and we already have plans for tonight. Some other time, maybe."

He nodded, pocketing his change. "Some other time."

"Myers! Order up!" yelled a chunky bald man in a folded white cap and grubby apron from the kitchen pass-through window behind her.

"Coming, Fred!" she called back and rushed away.

Peter slowly walked to the table, left a tip for her, and headed out to the parking lot.

CHAPTER TWO

Melinda fumbled with the keys to her apartment. She couldn't fit them into the lock. They rattled to the carpeted floor with a clang and she let out a growl of frustration. Her second try was more successful.

The entire afternoon had been a bit of a blur. Whenever she hadn't kept a tight leash on her thoughts, they seemed to wander from the task at hand to be filled with an image of perfect teeth, slightly wavy black hair, and a chiseled jaw uttering her name in a mellifluous baritone. And that dimple! Did God really make humans so perfect?

"Melinda ... Melinda." She jumped as the mental image suddenly shifted—black hair became dark brown, and nearly-black eyes transformed into piercing blue ones above the collar of a white captain's shirt. The perfect teeth didn't change, still smiling back at her warmly. "See you tonight, baby," he said.

"Robert," she whispered, and as the image faded she found herself staring at her own face in her hall

15

mirror. Even in the dim light, she could see the dark circles under her eyes and the beginnings of worry lines forming around her mouth, created by the habitual grim set of her lips. She studied herself, trying to remember a time when she looked happy. After a moment, she turned away in disgust.

As she entered the bedroom to change, Melinda ran her hand down the dress hanging from the door before putting it on. Sleeveless, with a sweetheart neckline and pleated waist, the retro design complemented the modern fabric perfectly. The gauzy silk chiffon overlay added just enough mystery without taking away any of the modesty.

She wondered what Robert would think of the skulls-and-roses look. With that thought, the world lurched into grayscale, and all those skulls made her think of death. The feeling of accomplishment faded as she zipped it up and disappeared into the bathroom.

Half an hour later, she emerged, her hair curled and up, her makeup perfect, and strappy black sandals on her feet. She silently packed up a worn picnic basket with two champagne glasses, a sandwich, and some fruit. The bottle that went in was real champagne for once—Peter's tip had been much more generous than she was used to, and she had felt like splurging a little.

Melinda wasn't sure why Peter had invited her out tonight. *Me and Robert.* Most of her customers didn't look at her twice. Well, there were always those guys that were especially rude—the kind that thought being a diner waitress meant that part of her job description was taking catcalls, pinches, and solicitations, regardless of the ring on her left hand. She had developed a pretty thick skin and a repertoire of biting comments that shut unwanted attention down fast. If that failed, Fred would roar out and send those customers packing—he had a zero-tolerance policy when it came to harassing his girls.

But Melinda wasn't used to someone expressing an interest in her. Like Peter. She wondered idly what movie he and his girlfriend were planning to see— then realized what she was doing and cut herself off with, "I'm such an idiot." She grabbed her black shrug and the picnic basket, then hurried out the front door—ignoring the transformed woman who passed by the hall mirror. She had dressed up for Robert, and no one else, just like she did every Friday night.

Her favourite park near the zoo was only a few blocks away on the Bow River. The sun was sitting on the skyline behind her as she found her special spot, spread out the blanket and picnic items, and sat down on a hill facing the water. Poplars in full leaf whispered in the slight breeze, and a pair of Canada geese bobbed in an eddy across the creek. She sat watching them as she ate her sandwich in silence, then took a sip of champagne. The mating pair were often there when she came. She had named them John and

Mary. Despite herself, she found a real smile on her face for the second time today.

Melinda watched Mary stand in the shallows and dip her head down into the water for a tasty morsel, while John kept a wary eye out from the bank. They alternated eating and watching, making quiet conversation with each other. A man appeared on the hill above them with a big Great Dane on a leash, startling the pair. They flapped away, scolding loudly, wings smacking the water as they fled.

Melinda sighed and turned to her companion.

"John and Mary are still here, Robert. Did you notice? Strange how they always come back. Just like us." She paused, chewing, then turned to the framed five-by-seven photo propped up on the blanket next to her, a flute of champagne balanced beside it. Tonight, however, the blue eyes and dimpled smile in pilot's uniform seemed somewhat accusing, and she couldn't look at him for long.

Melinda ignored her own guilty thoughts by gazing at the river. She grabbed the second glass of champagne, took a sip and murmured, "How do you like my dress?"

The next several weeks passed in pretty much the same routine as the last three years. On Saturday morning, Melinda tucked the sketch for this week's dress into her purse before work. On her way home, she took the bus to the fabric store to find fabric for it.

Starting Saturday evening, and continuing on through her two days off, she managed to get her dress pattern made, fabric cut, fit on the dress form, and basted together. By Tuesday night, she was making necessary adjustments and beginning to sew permanent seams with her machine.

Her small kitchen table was the hub of all her activity, with a dress form crammed into the space between it and the mountain of boxes in her living room. There was row upon row of them, each with a sheet of loose leaf taped to the side. After her weekly picnics in the park, each dress was carefully laid in its box on top of its pattern, added to a pile, and barely received another thought afterwards.

As the temperatures dipped from late summer warmth into the chill of early fall, the designs included longer sleeves or a woollen cropped jacket. Silhouettes varied from slender shift-dresses to pleated or gathered knee-length skirts. But always the colours were in monochromatic greys and blacks, with the occasional splash of red or vibrant pink thrown in.

Like blood and death, Melinda thought grimly once, when she had noticed the trend in her colour choices. But she didn't change her selections.

And often, as she crawled between her blankets, she would say to the man in the picture frame on her bed stand, "I'm making a new dress, Robert. You're going to love it."

CHAPTER THREE

Melinda blinked at seeing Peter at one of her tables a few weeks later. She knew her smile was more nervous than welcoming, but she really *was* trying. Fred caught a look at her through the pass-through window and rolled his eyes, letting out a loud puff of air. She glanced at him, tried to widen the smile a bit, and slowly approached Peter's booth, sucking in a deep breath and wiping her sweaty palms on her apron before speaking.

"Hello," she said tensely. "Iced tea again?"

Peter smiled warmly. "Hi, Melinda! I was hoping I'd see you here today. Iced tea is fine. Also, I brought something for you to look at." He patted a large brown book on the table that looked like it might be a photo album.

Melinda glanced around—it was a pretty slow lunch for a Tuesday. She might be able to take a look. But Fred had been watching her like a hawk, and he didn't like his girls sitting down with the customers, even for a few moments. A quick glance over her shoulder confirmed that he was watching her now with a furrowed brow in between prepping burgers and toasting sandwich bread.

"What is it?" she asked.

"Just some photos I have taken. Not much of a portfolio, but that's why I wanted to talk to you. I figured that if you like what you see enough, I would give you and Robert a deal on your wedding photos in exchange for helping me to accumulate some more advertising material. Or maybe engagement photos?" The grin he gave her looked more hopeful and boyish than she expected from his chiseled face.

She relaxed a little. "Robert and I already had our engagement photos done, sorry. I would love to see it, but I can't look at it while I'm working. Uh, can you stop by after work today?"

"Tell you what. I can't come back today, but I'll come by some other afternoon when you're off work, if that's okay. How about Thursday? Five-thirty, you said?"

Melinda nodded. "Sounds good." She strode off to get his drink order. She caught Peter winking roguishly at Fred as she was turning away. Fred let out another puff of air and started ignoring her so pointedly it was almost as bad as when he was watching her. Almost. She let herself feel a bit of gratitude toward the dark-skinned man.

22

As Melinda served him lunch, then cleared his dishes away, Peter kept trying to engage her in conversation. When she brought him an iced tea refill, he asked about Robert. She was surprised to find herself talking about him—really talking about him—for the first time in years.

"We met at, uh, the sports shop. By the skis," she said, shifting her weight. "He was looking for the 'perfect pair of downhill skis.' I was looking for the bathroom. I had my head up, looking for the washroom sign, and ran into him. Literally." She grinned wryly at the memory.

"Really? Guess that worked out for the best," Peter said, chuckling. "Anise keeps trying to convince me that we should go skiing at Whistler this winter, but I'm a little nervous about it. Do you ski?"

"No. Robert kept—I mean, keeps—promising to take me, but we, uh, never seem to have the time. He works so much, and when he is home, he just wants to relax. Not that I blame him. I don't know—I'm not a big 'outdoor winter sports' person."

"Growing up in Mumbai, I wasn't either, for some reason," Peter said with a straight face. She was shocked to hear an actual giggle coming out of her throat. How long had it been since she had laughed?

Peter's face cracked into a grin. "Ah, so you do have a smile in there somewhere." Peter clasped his hands and cracked his knuckles. "My work here is done."

Melinda's eyes widened, and for a moment she wondered if the reason he seemed so interested in her was because Fred had actually put him up to this. She glanced up at her boss, who had resumed scowling at her through the pass-through window, and pushed the thought aside. Fred would never hire someone to get her to smile—he would just fire her. She backed up as Peter started sliding out of the booth.

"I guess I better get back on the road—my work there is never done." Peter gave an exaggerated sigh.

She rang his order through the till and stood watching him until his cheerful "See you Thursday" was cut off by the door as it jangled behind him. Then she moved to clean up his table. He was already pulling out of the parking lot when she found his very generous tip under a napkin. "Keep smiling!" was scrawled across the napkin in a loose hand.

Her eyes followed the tail lights of the cube van as they turned out of the parking lot, a puzzled smile on her lips.

Peter did come back Thursday, but for lunch, and without the photo album. In fact, he seemed to be a regular customer that kept showing up in her section. The fact did not go unnoticed.

"What's with this guy that keeps showing up to visit ya, hun?" Sandra drawled one day as Melinda poured his iced tea. "Is he sweet on you, or somethin'?

You planning to lead him along the cherry lane? I've always thought chocolate ice cream much more interesting than vanilla, myself." She raised her eyebrows meaningfully. "'Specially for cherry-picking." She started collecting her order from under the heat lamps.

Melinda had never quite learned how to deal with this sort of teasing. "Stop it, Sandra. He's just a nice guy who is trying to get me to hire him as our wedding photographer. Nothing more. Besides, he has a girlfriend, so why would he be hitting on me?"

"Humph, if you say so. You know, when you're not glaring at folks like you're Morticia Addams, you've actually got something going on there, sweet thang." Sandra's overly-made-up eyes sparkled mischievously. Before Melinda could think of something—anything—to say in response, Sandra swept away with three plates stacked up her left arm and another in her right hand. Melinda gave her head a little shake and went to take Peter's order.

Peter made it a game to get Melinda to smile or laugh every time he visited. Rarely at a loss for a funny story, he would ramble about his girlfriend or stories about growing up in his crazy family in India, and he always succeeded in getting a warm response from Melinda—often more than once. He was pleased to note that her genuine smiles came quicker and more often with each succeeding visit.

However, despite their increasing rapport, Peter soon discovered that Melinda was not forthcoming with information about her own family.

"So, Melinda, tell me about yourself. Brothers or sisters?" he asked one day as she set his drink on the table.

"No," she replied, shifting her weight.

"And your parents? Where are they?"

Melinda's forehead furrowed, and her lips became firm. "My mom died when I was little, so I don't remember much about her. My dad died a few years ago. So now it's just me."

Peter mentally kicked himself for being such a prying idiot. No wonder she didn't ever talk about her family. And good luck getting her to bring out that beatific smile now. "I'm sorry to hear that. It must have been so hard for you to lose your dad."

Melinda sighed. "No need to apologize. It's not like it was your fault." She poised her pen to take his order.

Peter tried to regain the ground he had lost. "Well, at least you have Robert, right?" Her pinched look was not the response he was expecting.

"Yes, Robert. Of course." She smiled weakly. "What are you having for lunch today?"

He decided that the smile counted and ordered a large cheeseburger, relieved to move on to other topics.

Peter watched her swish away to call his order back and poke the chit on the little spinning wheel above the pass-through counter for the cooks. He couldn't quite get a handle on this girl. She seemed to clam up every time he asked her about herself, and after the conversation they just had, he began to understand why. He wasn't really sure why he felt this responsibility for her—like it might be his job to help her learn to live again—but at least now he knew some of what had dimmed the spark in her eyes.

He wondered if Preeti could be right that there really was no Robert. Maybe Melinda was completely and utterly alone in the world. Who knew what else was troubling her?

He felt a twinge inside of him at the thought. His eyes followed her perfunctory movements around the diner, and he determined to keep befriending her.

Maybe one day, he would be able to unravel the mystery that was Melinda.

Melinda rolled the circular blade of the rotary cutter along the edge of the pattern, neatly duplicating its shape in the fabric laid out carefully below. The kitchen table was not really big enough for cutting out most skirts, so she usually used the floor of her small galley-style kitchen. Despite the ache in her back, her mind wandered as she fell into the hypnotic rhythm of the process — trace the edge of a pattern piece with the razor-sharp blade, move the large, green mat which protected the linoleum to a new position below the fabric, repeat.

Making dresses was so simple. She loved the feel of the fabric and deciding whether this one or that one had the better drape for the project she had in mind. She loved taking a flat piece of cloth and making it into a beautiful item of clothing. She loved how subtle changes in the way a pattern was cut could drastically affect the final garment's shape. She loved how she knew exactly how to create a dress — you did step A, then step B, and so on until you were finished. And even if you made a mistake, it was very seldom unfixable with a little extra time and effort.

Not like life. Not like life at all.

As she cut, she heard her mother's voice, and her own chubby six-year-old hands seemed superimposed over the adult ones in front of her. *Make sure you lay the pattern out straight on the grain, or it won't hang right. Be careful, Melly, you don't want to cut yourself.*

They had made a little skirt for her to wear to school, red gingham with a black felt appliquéd poodle on it. She had loved working on that project with her mother, loved knowing that they had made something beautiful together.

Melinda remembered the first time she wore that skirt. All day, the feeling of wearing something she had made herself buoyed up her spirits in a way she had never experienced before. Her best friend had been completely amazed, and Melinda glowed in the admiration she could see in her friend's eyes. For the first time in her life, she felt really special.

Her insides were still effervescent on the bus ride home from school. It was while the bus was waiting at the stoplight to turn toward the subdivision where she lived that the unthinkable happened.

Melinda was sitting on the right side of the bus by the window. Looking absently through the glass, she spotted her mother's car waiting to cross the intersection and waved excitedly. Her mother spied her and waved back, smiling, before the light changed and the car slowly started accelerating.

That was the last time she saw her mother alive.

The pick-up that ran the red light exploded onto the scene like a bomb. The next few seconds were a cacophony of images and sounds that haunted Melinda in slow-motion nightmares for years to come—the blur of red and chrome, the ear-splitting squeal, the acrid stench of rubber sliding on asphalt, the jagged rending of crushing metal, the shattering glass spraying all over the pavement, her mother's green station wagon crumpled like a deflated accordion. She didn't even realize she had been screaming until she stopped to draw in a ragged breath.

Melinda had told her father that she hadn't seen her mother in the car after the accident, and he had been visibly relieved.

But she lied.

She wished she hadn't, and she thought by denying it she could forget the sight of her mother's broken body and lifeless eyes staring upward as her lifeblood seeped onto the vinyl seats.

Had her mother not been waving to her, would she have seen the truck speeding toward her? The thought reverberated inside Melinda's head for the thousandth time with the same gut-twisting ache. Some questions had no answers.

The cutter slipped off the edge of the mat, and she cursed aloud. A close inspection of the linoleum revealed no harm done, and she breathed a sigh of relief—which turned into a grunt of disgust when she noticed that she had nicked the fabric inside the edge of her pattern. After a few moments' examination, she decided she could work around it in the design, adjusted her mat and continued cutting.

Peter had been in the diner again yesterday, but he hadn't come alone. He had cheerfully introduced her to his girlfriend. However, Melinda's polite comment about having heard so many good things about the woman backfired. Melinda froze in mid-sentence when she sensed the sub-zero chill coming off of the ginger-haired, freckled beauty. There had been no friendly banter about Robert, Preeti, or anything else that lunch hour. Melinda had done only what was necessary to serve their table, and the few snippets of conversation she caught in passing were sharp-edged and terse. Finally, Anise swept out of the diner, leaving her soup and salad unfinished. Peter pushed his burger and fries away from him, half-eaten.

As Melinda came by to collect the plates, Peter managed a weak smile. "Thanks, Melinda," he said, then resumed gazing out the window with unfocused eyes.

Melinda kept glancing at him worriedly as she rang up his bill. She cautiously approached him. "Hey, are you okay?"

As he turned and focused on her, the glazed look in his eyes cleared.

"No, not really, I guess ... but I know I will be. Don't know when, but it will happen." He gave a snort of derision and looked down. "Anise just broke up with me." He exhaled loudly and shifted in his seat. "Okay, actually, no. I broke up with her, after she admitted to me that she had cheated on me." He looked back out the window. "Again."

Melinda slowly sank down in the booth across from him. "I'm ... I'm so sorry, Peter."

"Well, you'd think by now, I wouldn't be so surprised."

Melinda waited, not quite sure what he meant.

"Why do I have such stellar taste in women?" he said with a mocking laugh.

Melinda studied Peter's face, waiting.

"Well, I guess that's not important to you. We barely know each other. I'm sorry, Melinda, I shouldn't be dumping this all on you. I'm sure you have enough problems of your own to deal with."

"What do you mean by that?" she asked, startled.

Peter's eyes widened slightly. "Oh, uh, nothing. I mean, we all have our own problems, don't we? Mine is just choosing the wrong kind of women. Maybe I'll just give up dating altogether." He stared grimly at the blue Formica tabletop.

"Peter," Melinda said gently, "Not all women are like Anise. There are plenty of decent and loving girls out there looking for a wonderful guy like you. You're fun, you're caring, you're handsome … you have so much going for you. You just haven't found that special girl who will be 'The One' for you yet. That's all."

Peter looked up at her, his eyes murky black pools of sadness. She felt like she was drowning in them.

He let out a long breath. "Well, Melly—I mean, Melinda—if you see all that in me, I guess I won't give up yet. That Robert must be one amazing guy to have kept a girl like you. Lucky, too."

He always rolled his R's slightly, so "girl" sounded a bit like "gull." Melinda enjoyed listening to him speak so much it took her a moment to realize what he

32

had just said. When she did, she sat up straight, and she heard her father's voice muttering something about the tangled webs we weave.

"My mother used to call me 'Melly'," she said, hands suddenly busy smoothing her apron and tightening her ponytail, her eyes looking anywhere but at his.

"Oh, I'm sorry," said Peter hurriedly. "I won't call you that again, if you don't want me to."

"Melinda, Fred's giving you the evil eye," Sandra stage-whispered as she swept by with an arm full of dirty dishes. A quick glance over her shoulder confirmed Sandra's words, and Melinda jumped to her feet.

Peter was already fishing in his wallet for a few bills. "Keep the change," he said, his face grim, and slid out of his booth.

"Thanks," Melinda murmured. She pocketed the cash and grabbed his empty glass. He nodded and turned towards the door.

Without thinking, she placed a light hand on his arm to stop him. They were so close that she could feel the heat from his body.

"You can call me 'Melly' if you want to, Peter," she said, a little breathless to find his dark eyes looking down at her from such near proximity. She dropped her arm and took a step back. "And … please feel free to talk to me any time. About *anything*." Peter nodded, and she hurried away, chased by a loud snort from Fred.

The last piece finally cut, Melinda stood and stretched her aching back, then cleaned up the mess on the floor.

Why had she told Peter that? *Idiot!* But it had been so nice to have someone actually talk to her—really talk to her—the way Peter had been doing lately, and then to confide in her like a friend. How long since someone had done that? And how long since she had had someone to talk to who didn't stare back frozenly from behind a framed piece of glass?

You would have someone to talk to if you didn't push everyone away, the voice in her head accused.

As if presenting an indictment, the phone rang. Melinda glanced at the number and let it continue ringing. Eventually, the answering machine kicked on, and her own voice echoed as if from the bottom of a well, "This is Melinda. Leave a message." After the high-pitched squeal, Robert's sister came on the line. Her voice reflected the forced cheer of repeatedly talking to a machine instead of the actual person.

"Hey, Melinda, it's Nadia. Mom and I are coming to the city in a couple of days to go shopping, and we were wondering if we could meet up with you for lunch or something. We could come by the diner, if it would work better for you. Call me back and let me know. You know the number." She paused. "It would be really great to see you, Mel. It's been way too long." Another pause. "Okay, well. Call me." The phone clicked, and the machine squealed again.

Melinda ignored it, like she always did, and started pinning the bodice of her dress together on the dress form. Glancing up at the photo in the rustic wooden frame on her kitchen cabinet, she gave a start and pricked her thumb. Muttering to herself, she sucked on the droplet of blood that appeared and examined the spot. No more red seeped out, and she breathed a sigh of relief—she didn't want to have to stop working, and blood was so tricky to get out of wool.

Guiltily, she peeked back up at the engagement photo from the corner of her eye. Robert's brightly-smiling familiar face looked back at her, arm around a girl that looked like she could be Melinda's younger, happier, more carefree twin sister.

For a moment—just a fraction of a second—she could have sworn that the man in the photo had been Peter.

She shook her head and went back to work.

The Friday Night Date Dress

CHAPTER FOUR

Melinda sipped her tea, then returned the white stoneware mug to its saucer on the linen tablecloth and turned the page, her eyes riveted to the unfolding story of Moll Flanders. As Melinda lounged in the slightly-upscale Ambrosia, situated in the five-star L'Hotêl LaValle, she looked like a patron having a solitary supper before heading out for a party in her charcoal grey dupioni silk dress. At least, she hoped she appeared that way.

The slightly slubbed fabric of this Friday's dress had a wonderful sheen that she had just known was the perfect match for the slim, sheath-like silhouette of the design. A pleated drape crossed the bodice at a diagonal and was fixed in place over her left shoulder by a black-stained wooden spiral button. The drape fell in neat folds behind her to the knee-length hem of the skirt. The look faintly echoed an Indian-style sari, and she thought it was one of her more clever style adaptations.

Peter strode across the hotel lobby, camera dangling on his chest. He glanced through the decorative window panes of the hotel restaurant on his way by and stopped short. It took only a stuttering heartbeat to realize that he actually recognized the enchanting woman sitting by herself on the other side of the glass. Melinda's dark hair was piled on top of her head, and her pendant earrings swung alluringly like miniature pendulums against her cheek. She was so engrossed in the antique hardcover, she didn't notice him.

He nervously loosened his collar as he realized how absolutely stunning Melinda really was. Entering the restaurant, he approached her table in curiosity.

"Melinda?" he said when she didn't look up. "I hardly recognized you. You look amazing!"

With a small jump, she looked up and smiled, but started fidgeting with the edges of the pages as her smile faded.

"Peter. What are you doing here?" she asked evenly.

"Preeti hired me to cover a big shindig that *Fresh* is putting on in the ballroom." He lifted his camera. "I was just on my way back from the washroom when I saw you. And you? You're pretty dressed up for a date with Mr. Dafoe," he grinned, indicating the battered novel that she still held.

Melinda closed the book and placed it on the table, her face hot. She hated lying to him, but there was no way she was going to tell the truth. The lie was all she had left of Robert. The lie was the only thing protecting Peter.

Protecting herself.

"Robert's flight home was cancelled at the last minute, so he couldn't be here for our date tonight. Since I was already all dressed up, I thought I would at least go out for tea. I like this restaurant because it's quiet." *And I don't usually see anyone I know.*

"Oh. I'm sorry to hear that Robert couldn't make it. Having tea in a fancy restaurant does seem like the sensible thing to do in that situation." He grinned crookedly, and Melinda found herself smiling almost involuntarily … the same way that puppies and babies always made her smile.

"Hey, do you think Robert would mind if I invited you to hang out with me at the *Fresh* party? It would be nice to have someone I know to talk to. I'll have to take some photos throughout the evening, but other than that, we are free to mock the muck-a-mucks and divas of either gender as much as we want." He gave her another boyish grin, his eyes dancing.

"Um …" Melinda paused, warring with herself. The thought of a party with lots of people she didn't know, not to mention spending the whole evening with a man she only knew from work, made her utterly uncomfortable. But on the other hand, she realized that there was a fiercely lonely part of her soul that was hungry—no, ravenous—for genuine human interaction. She also knew if she went home now, she would spend the rest of the night wallowing in regrets.

"No, I don't think he would mind," she said, standing, gathering her wrap and purse, then leaving a few dollars on the table.

"Really?" Peter let out a breath. "Great! After you, m'lady." He grinned widely as he gestured toward the arched restaurant entrance with a flourish.

Melinda gave him a reserved smile in return as she swept past on four-inch heels that almost let her look him in the eye. *What are you doing?* nagged the familiar voice of doubt. She promptly squelched any misgivings. *Just having a bit of fun.*

In the ballroom, everything seemed glittery—the patrons in a stunning array of formal wear; the fabulous decorations on the tightly-packed round tables; the disco ball hanging over the hardwood dance floor. Even the stage was adorned with glittering silver garlands and floral arrangements. Melinda ran her hands down the muted grey silk of her dress and felt very self-conscious.

"Peter!" She tugged on his sleeve and yelled in his ear to be heard over the loud techno-dance music emanating from the speakers set up by the stage. "I don't think I quite fit in here."

He raised his eyebrows. "Are you kidding? You look perfectly enchanting. Like Audrey Hepburn crossed with Madhubala." He gave her the once-over approvingly.

She nodded uncertainly, confused by the unfamiliar reference, and continued to follow him. He looked casually stunning in black dress pants, an eggplant-coloured button-down shirt with the sleeves rolled up almost to his elbows, and a striped tie, no jacket.

Melinda watched a woman in an exquisite sequined floor-length, backless red dress stroll by on the arm of a black-tuxedoed man. The woman assessed Melinda in an instant—approvingly—before she passed by.

Melinda relaxed a little. Maybe Peter was right. And had he actually compared her with Audrey Hepburn? She blushed in delayed embarrassment at the compliment, glad that he couldn't see her face as she tailed him along the edge of the crowded room.

Peter found Melinda a place to sit near the back wall, away from all the high-traffic areas, and got her a cocktail to sip—virgin, at her request. He frequently returned to her table after roaming to various locations to capture the evening's highlights.

Dinner was already over, and people were milling around as servers cleared dessert dishes and refreshed coffee. The table was empty except for a bejewelled middle-aged woman that smiled blandly at Melinda before taking a long draught of garnet-hued wine. Melinda was relieved that the loud music made pleasantries next to impossible, even from just across a table. She smiled politely back at the woman, then turned away to watch the room at large.

Peter had just returned from one of his rounds and was about to sit next to her when he was hailed by a familiar voice.

"Peter! There you are!"

Melinda immediately recognized the open-R'd accent—Preeti. She tried not to gape at the gorgeous, perfectly-coiffed woman whose stilettos were clicking purposefully toward them. Caught in the diminutive woman's wake was a slim brunette that looked like she should be in a grey pencil skirt and holding a clipboard, not the floor-length gown she currently wore. She appeared even more businesslike than her boss.

"Oh, heya, Preeti," Peter said casually when she reached the table, lowering his camera. "Time for the show to start?"

"Yes, soon. I just want to make sure you take photos of a few specific people. Bonnie, please give him the list."

Preeti's shadow handed over an unsealed envelope. Peter took it with an amused expression.

"And how, dear sister, am I to know who these people are by only a name?"

Preeti gave an exaggerated sigh. "There are descriptions, too."

Peter pulled out the paper and scanned the contents.

"There have to be close to a hundred names, here, Preeti! Do you want me to memorize descriptions or take pictures?" He snorted in amusement. "I know— how about I make sure to take photos of all the really well-dressed people, okay? I'm sure that should about cover it."

Preeti glared at him. "Just don't miss any of them, alright?"

Bonnie clutched her employer's arm. "Time for the speeches, Preeti. You need to go."

"Right, thank you." Preeti took a step and stopped. "Well, Peter? Are you coming?"

"Of course—I'm right behind you." Peter rolled his eyes at Melinda. Preeti gave a satisfied nod and clicked away, Bonnie a step behind.

Peter tucked the folded list into his shirt pocket and gave Melinda's arm a quick squeeze. "I'll be back soon." He lifted his camera and strode off to a vantage point near the stage.

"Excuse me, I believe that's my seat," said a woman behind Melinda. Melinda apologized and stood, moving to a place near the wall from which she could watch the proceedings.

At the podium, a woman in a floor-length black gown introduced Preeti. Vivacious and stunning, Preeti swept forward and captured everyone's attention with a short speech about the relaunch of their magazine. After boisterous applause, she then welcomed many of the guests specifically by name before introducing the keynote speaker, an instructor from one of Canada's foremost design colleges.

Melinda listened, fascinated, to a leading educator in the field in which she had only self-educated, soaking up every drop of knowledge she could gather in a twenty-minute speech. Between Preeti's and Madame Bouvier's talks, Melinda gleaned that not only was Western Canada's hottest women's interest magazine refocusing on a new "timeless, edgy, and fresh" theme, but that there were several very famous fashion designers (and a few up-and-comers) in the room. After hearing that, she had eagerly peered around, unobtrusively trying to identify who was whom among the jewel-bedecked guests. She was delighted to recognize a few of her favourite designers in the crowd.

After the speeches, the dancing began. Peter had just managed to circle back to Melinda when Preeti caught up to him again.

"How's it going so far, Peter?"

"Just fine. You need to relax, sis."

He gently guided Preeti over to Melinda with a hand on her elbow. Melinda stepped away from the wall to greet her.

"You remember Melinda, right? I found her sitting in the hotel restaurant before the show, and since her date couldn't meet her, I insisted she come hang out with me." Peter winked at Melinda as if they shared a private joke.

Preeti looked confused for a moment, then recognition and a practised smile blanketed her face as she offered Melinda her hand.

"Of course. From the diner, right? Wow, what a fabulous dress! Where did you get it?"

"Uh, thank you. I, uh, I—had it made for me," Melinda stammered, uncomfortable at being the centre of attention.

"Really? It is stunning work," Preeti examined the dress closely with an appreciative eye. "Made by whom? Anyone here?" she asked, completely without pretense. In the shadows, Bonnie looked as though she was poised to take notes.

"Just a friend who sews," Melinda said, then changed the topic. "This is a great party. Peter said you were the driving force behind it. You must be very proud of how it all turned out."

Preeti beamed. "Thank you. Yes, it all turned out quite well, thankfully." She frowned and abruptly turned back to her brother. "Peter, that reminds me.

Did you get a photograph of the mayor and his wife? They look like they are getting ready to leave."

"Yes, *diidii*." He grinned at her. "I am pretty sure I have shot everyone in the room twice, and all the pretty girls at least double that."

Preeti glared at him, not appreciating his sense of humour. "A simple 'yes' would have sufficed," she snapped. "And it's my job to make sure everyone else is doing theirs."

"Never fear, Preeti." He patted her arm. "You will have plenty of photos to choose from for your press release and yearbook memories. Smile!" He raised his camera and aimed it at her. She quickly put on the practised smile before his camera flashed, gave him an exasperated look, and spun on her stilettos to check on something or someone else. Bonnie hurried to catch up to Preeti, who was already issuing instructions over her shoulder.

"Sisters." Peter shrugged at Melinda, a rueful grin on his face. "Gotta love 'em."

"You're lucky to have one with whom you are so close," Melinda replied wistfully.

"Well, she's okay most of the time," Peter said, glancing after his sister. "But sometimes she is a real pain in the backside."

Melinda laughed politely and shifted on her feet, the high heels pinching her toes. Her choice of footwear hadn't seemed so bad when her plans for the evening involved more sitting than standing, but she had spent most of the last couple of hours staying out of the way of legitimate guests—not an easy feat in such a crowded space. On the dance floor, "The Macarena" was just getting started, and the throbbing beat seemed in sync with the throbbing in her arches.

Some of the pain must have shown on her face, because Peter leaned in and touched her arm. "I'm pretty much done. You wanna get out of here? Go get some air?"

Melinda had been trying not to show how overwhelmed she was by the loud music, glittering lights, and crowds of people, but Peter seemed to notice anyway. She gave him a grateful smile and nodded.

"Just give me a minute," he said, then strode after Preeti. Melinda watched their quick exchange, after which Preeti nodded and Peter returned to her, his warm breath on her ear. "Okay, we're good to go."

Peter and Melinda strolled through an indoor jungle that encircled a large swimming pool, and before long found themselves in the semi-privacy of a little decorative pond area. The air was moist and warm and smelled faintly of chlorine.

Melinda gratefully sank onto a wood-slat bench and admired the scene before her. A rippling sheet of water flowed down an elegant glass elevator shaft, streaming from the high, vaulted ceiling down to the wishing pond in front of them. It was a perfect oasis of privacy on the edge of the busy hotel atrium. She kicked off her shoes and her toes wiggled in delight to be free from their constraints. *Strolling in four-inch heels isn't the best way to end a full day on your feet waitressing,* she smiled ruefully.

She abruptly realized that Peter had just asked her something.

"I'm sorry, Peter, I was thinking about something else. What did you say?" Melinda focused on the man standing before her.

Peter glanced down at her wiggling piggies and chuckled.

"I was just saying that Robert seems to be away a lot. No wonder you haven't gotten back to me about your wedding photos." He tossed a penny into the small pool and watched the ripples move lazily across the surface.

"Well, you were supposed to bring your photo album back, but I never saw it again. How am I supposed to know if you are any good?" She raised an eyebrow, a small smile playing on her lips.

"Yeah, sorry about that." He looked embarrassed. "I keep forgetting to bring it with me to work, and I can't leave it in the truck. I'll bring it to show you soon, I promise."

Melinda fidgeted with her black satin clutch. "How are things going in the move towards 'professional photographer,' anyway?" she asked.

"Well, I'm getting paid tonight!" he laughed, lifting the camera slightly. "It's a start, anyway." He turned and stared at the pool for a few moments. "Honestly, I need to get my portfolio together, because I'm never going to get steady work as a photographer if I can't show people professional work I've done."

"You seem to love doing it," she said. "What got you interested in photography?"

"My sister, actually," he said, and threw another penny at the pool, aiming at the exact spot where he had thrown the last one. He crouched by the edge of the shallow water and scooped out a handful of coins tossed by Wishers Past, then started tossing them back in one at a time.

Watching him from the bench, half-turned away from her, it was easy to study him. She wanted to drink him in, drink in his presence, his company. She had been lonely for far too long. A blood-red alarm started flashing somewhere in the back of her mind.

She ignored it.

"Preeti? How?"

"No, not Preeti." He looked up at her. "My twin sister, Kanti. She always used to fish old magazines out of the bin, just to look at the pictures. We children didn't have a camera—Papa didn't want to pay for developing the film, it was so expensive—so whenever she found a picture she really liked, she would cut it out and paste it into her scrapbook. Then she would use her fingers to pretend she was taking a picture of it. 'Click, gotcha' she would say, and laugh, framing the photo with her thumb and forefinger on each hand like this." Peter demonstrated, creating a miniature frame with his fingers, holding it up to look at Melinda with one eye squinting as if sighting a camera. He grinned when she blushed. "Pretty soon, we would do that wherever we went. If we saw something we thought was beautiful, or striking, or silly, or whatever, we would hold up our finger-frames and say 'Click! Gotcha!'"

Melinda found herself smiling along with Peter at the memory. "You've never mentioned Kanti before. Does she still live in India?"

"No," he said, eyes focused far in the distance. "She died when we were twelve. Malaria."

Melinda opened her mouth, working to get words past the lump in her throat. "I'm … so sorry, Peter. It sounds like you two were very close." Her heart, scarred by loss after loss, started to contract, pinching until her eyes started to well up. She brushed away a tear, hoping Peter hadn't seen.

"We were. She was probably my best friend, though I would never have admitted it. I think she knew, though." He tossed another coin in the serene pool. When he glanced back at her, Melinda just nodded, her sinuses burning from repressed tears.

"Before she died, I was sitting by her bed in our room. She looked so bad, you know? The doctor was just leaving, and my mother and father were speaking quietly to him by the door. Nobody would tell us kids how bad it was, but we knew it was serious." Peter shoved his fingers through his hair. "Then … I remember Kanti touching my hand and asking, 'Peter, do you think I'm pretty?'"

Peter stopped for a moment, tossing more coins, eyes fixed on the colliding ripples. When he spoke again, there was a catch in his voice. "I didn't know what to say—at twelve, you don't know how to tell your sister that you love her more than anyone else in the world. Just like she didn't know how to ask me … so I just held up my finger frames and said, 'Click! Gotcha!'" He looked down at his hands, fiddling with the few coins he still held. "After she smiled at me, she laid her head back and was gone, just like that." Peter sighed and locked eyes with Melinda.

She thought the lump in her throat might choke her.

"I still remember every detail of that picture of her, even though the camera was only in here," he said, tapping his temple. "She looked terrible, but she was so beautiful." He turned back to the pond to throw in another coin. "You know, I've never told anyone that before."

Melinda sniffed, and Peter looked back at her, surprised. "What's wrong?" he asked, dropping the remaining coins in the pond and coming over to sit beside her on the bench. He rested his hand lightly on her shoulder.

"It's just that …" she sniffed again, dabbing at her tears with a tissue, "I just feel sad for your loss."

"It's alright, Melly." Peter squeezed her shoulder, reassuring her with a comforting smile. "Kanti loved life more than anyone I've ever known. I miss her terribly—even now—but I can't stop living because she did. She would not want that of me." He chuckled. "In fact, she would probably come back from the grave to scold me soundly for even thinking of such a thing."

Melinda nodded, but somewhere inside of her a dam threatened to burst. She desperately applied some emotional cement and grasped at a subject change.

"About your portfolio …" She watched the waterfall, taking deep, controlled breaths.

"Yeah?"

"I, uh, have some special dresses that I have worn on dates with Robert. If it would help, I mean, if you wanted to, you could do a photo shoot of me in some of the dresses. As long as you let me have some prints for Robert—I think it would make a very lovely gift for him."

The sudden clack of a shutter release made her glance back at Peter, who was just lowering his camera.

"What was that for?" she asked.

"You looked so pretty just then, I had to take a picture." He laughed. "Click! Gotcha!"

Melinda chuckled in spite of herself.

"Don't worry, I'll give you a copy of that one for Robert, too. And I would love to do a photo shoot of you in all your pretty dresses," he grinned, looking more boyish than ever.

Melinda felt the urge to reach out and tousle his hair, but she kept her hand firmly on the purse in her lap.

They bantered about lighter topics, getting up and wandering around the atrium, until Melinda said she needed to go home.

Peter refused to let her call a cab and persuaded her to let him drive her home. As soon as he put the car into park, he jumped out and helped her out of the low vehicle, then walked her to the door of her apartment building.

She was just about to say a polite goodbye when he surprised her with a kiss on her hand.

"Thank you for making my night so delightful."

His fingers were warm and strong as they lingered around her own.

"I … it was so nice of you to invite me—thank you." She blushed, extracted her hand, and hurried into the building.

After her front door clicked closed behind her, Melinda collapsed back against it with a sigh, looking guiltily at the wall of dress boxes in her living room. When Peter had insisted on driving her home, she had not tried very hard to dissuade him. Now she berated herself for agreeing to spend the evening with him at all. Involuntarily, she clasped the hand he had kissed inside the other—it still tingled.

And now we're going to do a photo shoot, too? She banged the back of her head gently against the door.

"What am I doing?" she moaned.

Robert stared at her accusingly from the dining room. She couldn't meet his eye.

CHAPTER FIVE

$\mathcal{P}$eter fidgeted uncomfortably in a minimalist designer chair before a sizable glass desk in the fashion editor's office of *Fresh* magazine. Preeti murmured to herself as she flipped through an oversized photo album across from him.

It was disconcerting how the contents of the desk seemed to hang in thin air, suspended by an invisible force field. The room was all wide open spaces of white and orange and brushed stainless steel that could have come directly from an IKEA catalogue. The stark sterility of the office gave him the heebie-jeebies.

Preeti glanced up at him and he realized he was tapping his foot. He stopped with a sheepish glance at his sister. She resumed her inspection as though there had been no interruption.

The album contained the best shots from his session with Melinda. Images of the grey-eyed beauty in various poses, dresses, and settings flashed by as

Preeti turned pages, sometimes nodding, and occasionally pursing her lips in thought.

"Is this in the public library?" She indicated a photo where Melinda was poised on a library ladder, feinting to shelve a cloth-bound hardcover copy of *Jayne Eyre,* several other books clasped against her chest. Between the low scoop neck, filmy black blouse, and slim silhouette of the grey jumper she wore, "sexy librarian" didn't begin to cover the look.

Peter had charmed the actual librarian into giving up her dark-rimmed glasses for the shot. The final image had Melinda's grey eyes peering over the rim of the glasses directly into his own, lips slightly parted as if inviting a kiss. Thinking of those lips, his thoughts started wandering in a direction he couldn't afford to go, and he jerked back to the present.

"Yes. I have a friend that works there, and he let us shoot in the stacks for about an hour one afternoon. The light was great at that time of day. I love the whole Gothic feel of the place, too."

"Very creative how you used the intellectual setting to showcase such an alluring design, showing a woman with beauty and brains. I also love the ones you did at the Laundromat—I confess, I never would have thought of that location. But it totally works."

Preeti paused and angled the book to get a better look at one particular photo, then turned the book toward him. "Where was this taken?"

It was the shot of Melinda in the grey silk dress he had snapped at L'Hotêl LaValle's terrarium, which he explained to her. Personally, it was his favourite photo of them all—the look on her face was so open and vulnerable. It was a look he had never caught there at any other time.

Preeti merely turned the album back toward her, lifting the top edge to get a better view, and studied the photo again. Suddenly, she looked up and announced, "That's it, she's hired."

"'*She's* hired?!'" Peter spluttered. "For what? I thought this was about *me* getting hired?"

"Oh, nonsense. I always knew I was going to hire *you*. I just wanted to see you take some initiative in the process."

Peter was both flabbergasted and outraged. His big sister had always been a bit bossy, but *really*!

Preeti tapped her fingernail on the photo. "But this girl … I can admit when I am wrong, and this is one of those times. She has quite a striking quality to her that I didn't see at first. And these dresses!" She flipped back through the album again as she spoke, still trying to catch details she had missed. "I absolutely must know who this designer friend of hers is. These designs are exactly the type of 'timeless, edgy, and fresh' look that we are going for. I want to do a complete spread with her in these, and feature her designer friend." Preeti was on a roll, and didn't notice Peter trying to get a word in edgewise. "Just think, a designer of this calibre living right here in Calgary! This could be a cover story! What is it, Peter? Stop stuttering like an orangutan and spit it out!"

Peter's glare could have frozen lava, but he jumped in. "That's just it. I think that *she* is the designer."

"What?" Preeti looked up sharply.

Peter told her what he had observed when helping Melinda carry her things into the apartment after the photo shoot day—Melinda protesting all the while. All of them pointed to Melinda as the designer—the dozens of stacked boxes with sketched designs tacked on them, the sewing machine, paper patterns, and the dress form with a partially-finished gown on it. He didn't mention that he had also noticed the framed engagement photo with the smiling couple, or the dusty wedding invitation sitting on the counter for a wedding that supposedly occurred between Melinda Myers and Robert Clarkson nearly three years ago. That part of the puzzle he was still chewing on. At least he now knew Robert was real, after all.

Preeti's eyes widened with excitement. "This could be big. Really big. 'Diner waitress turns model and designer.' Everyone loves a good Cinderella story. She could become iconic! Give my assistant her phone number so we can get her in here right away."

Peter held up his hands to stop the onslaught. "Preeti, slow down! I'm not so sure she is going to want to have her photos and dresses featured in your magazine. She won't even take credit for making

58

them, for crying out loud! If you come at her with guns blazing and the spotlight already on, she'll run so fast you won't even see the shadow of the dust."

Preeti blinked and her brow furrowed. Her nails rat-tatted on the glass desktop and she looked past him with narrowed eyes, chewing on her lip. Peter recognized that look. She was not going to let this go.

Preeti met his gaze, the request in her eyes backed by determination as hard as steel.

No wonder she got this job, he thought, already feeling himself yield.

Finally, he sighed. "Fine. I'll talk to her. But I'm not going to promise anything."

Preeti's face broke open in a victorious grin. Peter tried not to let it irritate him.

"Wonderful! I know you will do your best." She closed the portfolio album. "Is it okay if I hang onto this for now?"

"Sure. Knock yourself out," he said resignedly, standing as she did the same. Apparently, the interview was over. He swung into his leather bomber-style jacket and slung his worn leather messenger bag over his shoulder. He headed for the glass doors.

"Let me know by Friday," Preeti ordered.

"Not promising anything, Preeti," he tossed over his shoulder just before the door closed behind him.

Preeti watched her brother's back retreating down the hallway. She couldn't help but smile once more as she patted the brown album.

One way or another, this girl would be in Preeti's magazine.

She just didn't know it, yet.

Melinda sat at her kitchen table, sewing machine pushed toward the wall, flipping through the album of eight-by-tens before her in amazement. Peter sat on the apartment's only other seat across from her, directly under the studio shot of a smiling couple. He watched her pensively as she examined his work, displaying an unusual amount of nerves. Melinda might have shown more empathy if her own anxiety level wasn't through the roof. She always felt that way when she knew she had to do something unpleasant.

At the moment, telling Peter she couldn't see him anymore was about the most unpleasant thing she could think of doing.

"These are amazing, Peter. Preeti's right—you are an extremely talented photographer."

Her memory of the photo shoot was a collage of hauling dresses and photographic lights around to various unlikely locations, changing her clothes and hairstyle more times than she could count, and contorting into what felt like the most unnatural poses, but which looked completely natural and flattering in the photos before her. She could hardly believe the relaxed, happy, beautiful girl in the album was really herself. That day spent with Peter had been one of the most enjoyable she had had since … since Robert—

"So, I got the job," Peter said.

Melinda nodded. "I'm not surprised." She flipped pages slowly, mesmerized.

"Melly, tell me the truth—did you make those dresses?"

Melinda drew in a sharp breath and looked up. He was leaning forward, elbows on his knees, his dark eyes piercing her soul. She turned her head and avoided his gaze for a few moments. Finally she sighed and sat back, meeting his eye.

"Yes," she said, resignation in her voice.

"Did you design them, too?"

"Yes."

"Well, that's great! They are all beautiful, and you obviously do a great job. And that's just coming from an uneducated schmuck like me. Why didn't you say so before?"

Melinda got up and started fiddling with the pins of the frock on the dress form. The fabric was printed with whimsical songbirds on a background of emerald green and lemon yellow.

Green? Birds?! The alarms in her head were screaming as she realized for the first time how dramatic a departure the fabric choice was from her typical fare. She remembered the twitter-pated euphoria that had engulfed her as she floated around the fabric store that week, and had no doubt of the cause. It was definitely time to cut ties while she still could … for Peter's sake.

"I didn't tell you before because …" She sighed and turned towards him. "Because of what you are doing now. I hate it when people make a big deal about me. I'm not a big deal. I just sew because … well, because it's what I do. It keeps me sane, and gives me something to do while Robert is away."

"I know you don't think so, but you actually *are* kind of a big deal," Peter said, half-smiling, but with an intense look in his eyes. "Did you see those photos? I didn't have to use a lot of photographic skill to make you look fabulous. You're a natural model, and I'm not the only one who believes that. Preeti loves those photos so much, she wants to hire you."

Melinda gaped at Peter. "Me? What for?"

"Well, to model. But specifically, to model your own designs. She wants you to be the featured designer in their next issue."

Melinda felt like her brain had just experienced whiplash. She sank slowly onto the thrift-store vinyl chair, completely at a loss.

"This could be a great opportunity for you." His black eyes sparkled like there were stars in them. "You wouldn't have to work at the diner anymore. Preeti has a ton of connections in the fashion industry, and she could help you get set up doing this for a living. Wouldn't you like that?"

Melinda touched her fingers to her temples. Nothing made sense. "Um, yes. I mean, No! I'm not a designer. And I'm not a model! Is this some kind of a joke?" She suddenly sat up, frowning.

"This is no joke, Melinda! You are a very beautiful woman, and it's time you know that Robert isn't the only man—uh, person—who thinks so. And look around! How many dresses do you have in that room? Fifty? A hundred?"

"One hundred forty-eight," she said mechanically. If what he was saying was true, this could be her chance to start over, leave the past behind. She could—

"What?! You see? You *are* a designer! And you create exactly the look that *Fresh* wants. Preeti wanted to talk to you herself, but I thought you might take it better from me."

His words cemented her resolve. She had to stick to her original plan. Working with *Fresh* would mean working with Peter, and that absolutely must not be allowed to happen.

Meeting his eyes, she wanted desperately to tell him she would do it, to not see disappointment etched on his beautiful face, but instead—

"I—I can't," she almost whispered.

"You can't what? Model? Be in the magazine?"

"None of it. I can't be in the magazine, or be a designer." She forced herself to look at him. "And … I can't see you anymore." Her resolve nearly crumbled when she saw the stunned look on his face.

"What?" Peter frowned and shook his head slightly. "Melinda, you don't have to be in the magazine. No one is going to make you do anything you don't want to do. But—you don't want to be friends with me anymore? What did I do?"

Melinda looked away, barely keeping the dam on her emotions intact.

"I just can't, Peter," she said in a low voice and studied her hands. "I'm sorry. I wish … things were different." She wiped away a drop of moisture that escaped her control. "Thank you for the photos— they're lovely. But … I need you to leave now. Please?"

After an endless, unbearable silence, she heard him get up and scoop his leather jacket off the chair. Unexpectedly, he squatted directly in front of her, startling her. She desperately wanted to look away from the pain in his bottomless black eyes, but couldn't.

"Hurting you was the last thing I ever wanted to do, Melinda. Whatever I did, I'm sorry. I wish—" he broke off. She sucked in her breath as he raised a hand as though to caress her cheek. It hovered inches from her face for a few moments before he slowly lowered it. She dropped her gaze to her hands again, afraid of what emotions might show in them. "I'll go for now, but I'm not abandoning you. I'm your friend, and you won't get rid of me that easily." When she didn't respond, he sighed, got up, and headed toward the door.

After the apartment door clicked shut and the sound of his shoes descending the stairs had faded, the dam burst. She wept a flood, pacing back and forth in the small space allowed by her tiny kitchen floor.

It was for Peter's own protection. She knew that. But that didn't make it hurt any less.

"Peter, I'm sorry," she sobbed. "You'll never understand, I know that. It's just that … everyone who gets close to me ends up—" she whispered, "dead."

Much later, when shuddering sighs were all that remained, she ran a glass of water and leaned against the counter to drink it. Her eyes fell on the album still laying open on the table.

The girl in the photograph—adorned in a retro skulls-and-roses print dress and surrounded by an opulent display of actual roses—never even blinked. She was too engrossed with gazing at the person behind the camera with a wide, unguarded smile.

"Hello, TransCan Airlines. How may I direct your call?"

"Uh, hi. My name is Peter Surati, and I am trying to get in contact with a pilot named Robert Clarkson. Would you be able to leave him a message for me?"

"One moment please." Peter waited patiently, listening to keys clicking on the other end of the line. "I'm sorry, sir, but there is no one by that name in our employee database. Are you certain that he works for our airline?"

"Well," Peter hesitated. Suddenly he was not so certain. From the photo he had seen of Robert in a captain's uniform at Melinda's place, he knew he certainly had worked for that airline at one point. "He may have moved to a different airline, I suppose. Could you do an historical records check for me? It is extremely important that I get in contact with him."

"I'm sorry, sir, I don't have access to those files. I will put you through to the Human Resources department."

"Thank you."

After listening to a jazz rendition of Andrew Lloyd Webber's "Memory" for about thirty seconds, a polite male voice came on the line.

"TransCan airlines, Andrew speaking. How may I help you?"

Peter explained his reason for calling again.

"I'm sorry, sir, those records are confidential."

Peter knew that laying on the charm would not work quite so well with a man as it would have with a woman. He tried a different approach.

"Mr. Clarkson has defaulted on a debt, and I represent Avery Collection Services. We are simply trying to track Mr. Clarkson down for our client."

The line was silent for a moment. "I can't give you any personal information about our employees. I am sorry I cannot be of more help."

Peter took a breath to keep from raising his voice in frustration. "Can you at least do a search to tell me how long ago he left your company? That might assist me in finding where he went next."

A pause on the line. "Let me check with my supervisor," Andrew said, and before Peter could reply, he was listening to an alto saxophone wail out an old Michael Bolton ballad. Blissfully, it was only a few seconds before the polite Andrew was back on the line. "Mr. Surati?"

"Any luck?" Peter asked. Too late. The lyrics to "Sometimes When We Touch" started trailing through his brain, picking up right where the canned music had been cut off. He hated when songs got stuck in his head like that—especially the cheesy ones.

"That shouldn't violate any policy. One moment, please." Keys clicked, then went silent. Peter realized he was humming while he waited, and started cursing silently in Hindi to obliterate the rest of the words. Andrew was mumbling indistinctly as he scanned the file, and Peter thought he caught the word "deceased." Then, "Uh, Mr. Robert Clarkson has not worked for us for nearly three years. I can't tell you any more."

"Wait, did I hear you say he is deceased?" asked Peter. There was only silence. "Andrew?"

"Yes, sir," came the reluctant reply.

"You're certain?" Peter asked, stunned.

Andrew sighed. "Yes, sir. He died on December 14, three years ago. Is there anything else I can help you with, sir?"

"Uh, no. No, thank you. Have a good evening."

"Good evening, sir." The line went dead.

Peter put the phone down and rubbed his chin. What to do now? Was Robert really dead? It made sense in a way, since he never seemed to show up with Melinda. But … maybe it was the wrong Robert Clarkson. If only Melinda would talk to him, he wouldn't have to try to go through the back door to know for sure.

After leaving her so upset, he had told himself it was foolish to worry, that she had Robert to look after her, but still thought it would be best if he could touch base with the man. But now … what if she didn't have Robert? And if she wasn't worried about a jealous fiancé, then why did she shut him out?

Without much hope, he punched in Melinda's phone number again. She probably still wouldn't pick up, but he didn't know what else to do at this point.

CHAPTER SIX

Three years ago to the day, Melinda and Robert waited anxiously in the hospital corridor as the doctor slipped silently out of her father's room and closed the door. Nurses and orderlies going about their duties filled the sterile space with soft rustles and muted murmurs. In the cancer ward, there weren't many loud noises, unless they were groans of pain or suffering.

The doctor was an older gentleman with a reassuring, grandfatherly manner, but right now, his face was grim.

"I'm sorry I don't have better news," he said. "The cancer has progressed more rapidly than we expected. Your father is fighting hard, but he doesn't have much left to fight with. I'm afraid you need to expect the worst."

Melinda's hand covered her mouth, her eyes wide and filling with tears. Robert put his arm around her shoulders to steady her.

"How long, Dr. Bezz?" he asked.

"It's possible that he has several more days. However, he most likely will not last another night. All we can do now is to try and keep him comfortable."

Herman Myers had been diagnosed with liver cancer only three weeks before after a history of robust health. He had gone into the emergency room with flu symptoms that seemed especially severe. By morning, he was told that he had advanced liver cancer, and there was very little that could be done at that point.

The weeks since the diagnosis had been a blur. Melinda spent most of her days—and nights—at the hospital. Others had come and gone with well-wishes for Herman's recovery, but only Robert's family and Pastor Ralph and Edith McKay understood how dire the situation was.

Robert's sister Nadia had come to see Melinda every few days. Pastor Ralph had come as often as he could, but Herman was seldom lucid enough for a visit. Edith often came, too, just to make sure that Melinda was eating and to give her a grandmotherly shoulder to cry on.

Robert had taken the week off of work to let Melinda get some rest. Despite the morning's news— or maybe because of it—he had insisted she go home. His concerned face and her exhaustion finally convinced her. However, she only managed a few hours' sleep before worry woke her again.

After splashing some water on her face and running a brush through her hair, she went straight back to the hospital. When she got to her father's room, a nurse was just coming out with a clipboard that she dropped in the slot by the door. She gave Melinda a consoling look, then moved on to the next patient's room. Melinda gulped, then leaned against the wall for a few moments, steeling herself for what she might find.

When she entered the hospital room, Robert jumped up from a chair by the bed to greet her. She gave him a questioning look.

"Any change?"

Robert shook his head. "He hasn't stirred all afternoon, but his vitals seem to be holding steady."

Melinda nodded and turned toward her father. The frail man on the bed seemed a cruel and ghostly caricature of the man who had been her pillar for the last sixteen years.

Herman's eyelids didn't even flicker as she sat down beside him and touched his hand. The skin was yellowed and paper-thin, crumpled like a glove that was too big for the hand it covered.

"Hey, Dad," she said. When there was no response, Robert squeezed her shoulder and pulled over another molded plastic chair next to hers. It made a horrible scraping noise on the tile floor that grated at her already-raw nerves.

The morphine they were administering to keep Herman comfortable made him sleep most of the time, but she and Robert still kept their voices low as they talked. They didn't say much, and when they did, it was always of the lightest topics possible—things far removed from the one thing their thoughts were centred on. Robert left and returned with a tea from the hospital cafeteria for her and a coffee for himself. Neither one of them would go home to sleep tonight.

After a nurse came in to check Herman's vital signs, he stirred. His eyes opened and turned, unfocused, on his daughter, who grasped his hand in both of hers.

"Dad, can you hear me? I'm here. Robert is with me."

"Mindy? I'm … cold."

Melinda glanced at Robert, and he jumped up to get another warm blanket from the nurse's station. She turned back to her father, grieving at how his once-commanding face now sagged slack and uncertain. Suddenly, his features firmed and his steel-grey eyes looked right into Melinda's face.

"I'm sorry I'm going to miss your wedding, honey. I really wanted to give you away."

Tears slid down Melinda's face, but she ignored them. "It's okay, Dad. At least you'll get to sit with

Mom for the ceremony." Saltwater brined her tongue as she gently smiled.

He weakly gripped her hand back. "Robert is a good man. At least I can go, knowing that you will be looked after."

"Daddy?" she whimpered, though she hadn't called him that for years. "I don't want you to go." Her body shook with sobs and her head dropped to her chest. She looked up in surprise as she felt his other hand on hers, IV tube taped to the back, but the palm warm and reassuring against her skin.

"You'll be all right," he said, patting her hand. Robert had returned with a nurse, who was arranging a warmed flannel sheet over the several other blankets already covering the man. His gaze flicked around and encompassed Robert. "You'll be all right. Always remember I love you."

With that, his eyes closed and he slipped into unconsciousness. By morning, his body had been moved to the hospital morgue.

She had been so thankful that Robert had been there to help with all the funeral preparations and paperwork that ensued. She went through the next week in a dry-eyed trance. Robert was there through it all, holding and comforting her, not making her talk, nor offering platitudes like so many of the well-wishers who came to the funeral or sent flowers or cards.

But when the funeral was over and the people stopped coming, Robert had to go back to work. Melinda didn't want to be left alone, but she knew it was necessary.

Robert wasn't home much for the next two weeks and the days seemed to drag by. She went back to work, too, grateful for the distraction it provided. But her shift always ended too soon, and she would come home to a quiet, empty apartment, with nothing to do but remember. Reading or watching television only depressed her further—she needed to *do* something.

Melinda and Robert hadn't had time to deal with any of her dad's stuff, so they just moved it from his house into a storage unit. One night after work, she took the bus to the unit looking for … something.

Melinda threw up the rolling door and surveyed the stacks of assorted boxes and furniture. With a sigh, she started poking through the boxes nearest the door, not even sure why she was there.

In the third box, she found the little gingham poodle skirt she had made with her mother—and she knew why she had come. With sudden focus, she rearranged the piles, searching for her mother's sewing supplies. She knew they were in here somewhere—she remembered packing them into the moving truck.

Before long, her efforts were rewarded. She borrowed the office's phone to call a cab to come pick her up, along with her mother's sewing machine and a box of fabric and patterns.

Two weeks after her dad's funeral, Melinda prepared to greet Robert after five days away. Her hair and makeup were partly done, and she was already dressed in her surprise for him—a dress finished just that afternoon. Opening her favourite lipstick, she was startled by the jangle of the telephone. Glancing at the clock, she thought it must be Robert—maybe his flight came in early, and he was calling to let her know.

"It's Nadia. Turn on the news—now."

Confused, Melinda turned on the TV, still holding the phone. A newscaster was reporting that a commercial plane had gone down over the mountains only an hour before. She slowly sank onto the couch, the phone falling from her hand.

As the flight number was announced, she uttered a soundless, "Oh, no." She was still sitting on the couch two hours later, eyes riveted to the news broadcast in shock, when Robert's mother Valerie called her. Robert had not been among the survivors.

Melinda was jolted back to the present by the shrill ring of the telephone. She didn't stir from her chair as the answering machine kicked on and Nadia's voice came on the line.

"Hi, Mel. Just thinking of you today. I know it's the day you lost your dad. I just wanted you to know that I'm still here if you ever want to talk. Oh, uh, Jason and I will be in the city on the weekend, and we hoped you would join us for dinner." Pause. "I miss you, girl, and I love you. Please, please call me back."

Immediately, the phone started ringing again. It wasn't like Nadia to be this persistent. Tightening her jaw, Melinda went into the bathroom to brush her teeth, but froze in mid-brush when she heard Peter's voice on the line.

"Hi, Melinda, it's Peter. Please pick up. I know you're there. I stopped by the diner earlier, and Sandra told me you were home sick."

That was true—she had taken the day off, as she did every anniversary of her father's passing.

There was a pause for a few seconds. "Melly, I really want to talk to you. I'm—well, I'm worried about you. Whatever you're going through right now, you don't have to do it alone. You know that, right?" He sighed into the phone. "Call me back when you get this. Please."

Melinda dropped the toothbrush into the holder and crawled under the covers. This was the second Friday in a row that the emerald-and-lemon bird-covered dress hung in a half-finished, pinned state on the dress form. She hadn't touched it since the night she sent Peter packing.

In fact, she didn't know if she would ever sew again.

The Friday Night Date Dress

CHAPTER SEVEN

Peter turned the key in his mail box to lock it, then started rifling through the handful of envelopes, bills, and flyers. The latest issue of his photography magazine had come, and he relished the thought of perusing it over a cup of coffee as he headed toward the apartment stairs. On the third step, he paused — there was an envelope with his name and address written in Preeti's hand, but with *Fresh Magazine* printed in the return address. Using his pinky finger as a letter opener, he jaggedly ripped open the envelope and pulled out a cheque. A handwritten note from his sister said simply, "For photography services rendered."

Confused, he looked in the envelope for a letter or some other explanation, but it was empty. He had already received payment for the re-launch gig, and had not yet done any other work for the magazine, so he had no idea what this cheque could be for. Some kind of advance, maybe?

Peter speed-dialled Preeti's cell number and held his phone to his ear with his shoulder as he unlocked the apartment door and entered. He tossed his keys and the other mail on a side table so he could grab the phone with his hand. When he heard her greeting, he started in right away.

"Hey, Preeti, wh—?" He cut off when he realized he had her voicemail.

"—reached Preeti Anderson's cell phone. Leave a message, and I'll call you back as soon as I can."

"Hey, Preeti, just got this cheque from *Fresh*, but I'm not quite sure what it is for. Give me a call, okay?"

Peter hung up, tossed the cheque on top of the pile of mail, then went rummaging through the refrigerator for leftover takeout.

The next morning was Monday. December second.

In India, December had been a welcome reprieve from the heat of summer and the wetness of monsoon. However, since moving to Calgary, Peter disliked December. Not only was the weather becoming intolerably cold—penetrating even the warmest of winter gear to chill his Mumbai-grown bones—but the Alberta air was always dry, and became even more-so when the little remaining humidity crystallized into snow. And was there ever a lot of snow.

There seemed to be more of the white stuff than usual this year—or so the locals said. He almost wished for the loosely-regulated traffic flow of Mumbai to driving these wintry city streets. Not only must he continually plow through drifts to make his deliveries, the constant in-and-out of the warmed truck made his nose run and his throat crack.

He dropped the box from *Fresh* on the receiving desk of Chapters bookstore. The receiving clerk smiled as she signed off with his digital pen. "Cold enough for ya?" she asked as he stamped his feet. It was a familiar question, and he had come to learn it was the polite way that Canadians had of commiserating about the weather without appearing to complain about it.

"If I never saw 'freezing' again, let alone 'twenty below,' it would be too soon," Peter replied good-naturedly.

Laughing, the curly-haired woman handed back his digital signature pad and pen and grabbed a utility knife to split the plastic binding on the box. "Stay warm!" she shouted after him. He waved in response to this other oft-heard greeting and disappeared through the heavy metal door, a blast of cold air hitting his face.

"Awesome," said the curly-haired woman to no one in particular as she opened the box to the latest edition of *Fresh*. "I've been waiting for these."

She grabbed a stack and slit the plastic straps that bound the bundle together. The glossy cover photo caught her eye. "The Surprising Melinda Myers— From Fashion Oblivion to Centre Stage" was the headline that accompanied the full-page photo of a gorgeous young woman with dark hair and penetrating grey eyes in an amazing black sheath dress.

The receiving clerk took a few moments to flip to the title story and ogle over the dresses that were the brainchild of the up-and-coming local designer. Idly, she wondered what the chances were of ever meeting Ms. Myers, and where she could find a dress like that one with the red embroidered rose-and-thorn pattern for the staff Christmas party. At another shout from her boss, she jumped to her feet, grabbed the box of magazines and went out to stock shelves.

Melinda rushed into the diner on Tuesday morning and stamped the snow off of her boots. She was late, and she knew it. She hoped Fred wouldn't notice.

Sandra was huddled over a magazine laid out on the counter, wet rag idle in her hand as she whispered excitedly with Margot, one of the morning line cooks. Melinda frowned. Fred's wasn't due to open for another twenty minutes, but that still didn't leave time for the opening staff to dally with small talk. As

Melinda passed, the two women stopped chattering and looked up at her in a most peculiar way.

"Mornin', Melinda!" Sandra chirped. "Did you have a good weekend?"

"Same as always," she replied, her face stony as she swept by the counter. Out of politeness, she forced herself to inquire, "You?"

"Oh, you know. It's always a little crazy running the kids here, there, and everywhere, 'specially in this weather. I survived, though. 'Course, I don't think any news I have could compare to yours, no matter *what* you pretend, Miss 'Ain't-Nothing-Happening-Here'."

Melinda stopped in her tracks, confused. "What do you mean?"

"Why, *this*, sweet pea, and don't act like you're not excited about it. I swear, sometimes you wouldn't take a compliment if the good Lord Above came and handed it to ya wrapped in a pretty red bow. This is amazing!" While Sandra talked, she shoved the open magazine into Melinda's face.

On catching sight of herself—*Peter's photos!*—in full glossy with tiny paragraphs and flowing subtitles on each page, Melinda's mittens, purse, and sneakers all crashed to the floor. She snatched the magazine from Sandra and hastily flipped through page after page of herself posing in her dresses, then looked at the front. *Fresh*. Of course.

"Myers, I need to talk to you," growled Fred, appearing through the pass-through window. "My office. Now."

Melinda handed the magazine back to Sandra in a stunned daze and shuffled back to Fred's tiny office as if in a trance. The desk, which was built into one short end of the small rectangular room, was neat and tidy, office supplies contained in utilitarian organizers, with a neat stack of file folders in one corner. Fred closed the door behind her and wiped his hands on the mostly-white apron around his waist. At this time of day, there hadn't been much to smear it yet.

Fred ran a hand over his bald head, looking extremely uncomfortable. "Myers, I've given you chance after chance. You were doing pretty good there for a while, you know? I thought this was going ta work out after all. But lately, you been moping 'round here like you're on a solid diet of lemons and Prairie Oysters. What's going on? You feeling okay?"

Melinda shook her head, eyes still focused on some place far in the distance. "No, I'm not. In fact, I feel quite ill. I think I'd better go home." She wasn't exaggerating—her head was spinning so fast, she sank into the rolling office chair in a daze. The scowl on Fred's face slid into a frown of concern. He whipped off his apron, hung it on a peg, and grabbed his coat and keys.

"I'll take ya home, then. You do look pretty awful. Caught that flu that was going 'round, didja? Why'd

84

ya even come inta work today?" He opened the office door and hollered toward the kitchen.

"Wong!" Margot's head popped around the corner. "Finish setting up for me. I'm taking Melinda home. Be back in half an hour." Margot gave an efficient nod and disappeared into the bowels of the kitchen again.

Melinda protested that she could get herself home, but Fred insisted, and she relented. She really did feel physically ill at the moment, and the thought of fighting her way home through all those drifts— against the wind, this time—followed by the morning crush in transit … she couldn't do it. She stumbled out of the office after him.

"Hey, Melinda, where can I get a dress like this one?" Sandra waved the magazine and poked it with a red-lacquered fingernail as Melinda passed the counter. "My daughter is graduating this year, and she would look fabulous in it."

"Back to work, White!" Fred shouted as he marched briskly through the doors, car engine already revving as he punched the Command Start button on his key fob. "And call Lacey to cover!"

"I—I don't know," Melinda said, practically fleeing through the door behind Fred. The cheerful clang of the bell chased her out with its mocking laughter.

"Preeti! What were you thinking?!" exclaimed Peter, shaking the magazine in his sister's face. They were once again in the uncomfortable white office. Peter was leaning on the glass desk behind which his sister sat—unperturbed, hands folded, smiling up at him infuriatingly. "Melinda didn't agree to this! I didn't agree to this! This isn't even legal!"

"You had her sign the standard modelling release form, did you not?"

"Yes, but—"

"Then she didn't have to agree to it. The article may have been more interesting had she allowed herself to be interviewed, mind you, but her photos can be used in any way that you want."

"But I didn't agree to this! Those are *my* photos, Preeti. And I would never have let you use them without Melinda's consent!"

"You're an employee of *Fresh* now, aren't you? Okay, subcontractor, not employee. Any photos you submit to us are free to be used in our magazine."

"I didn't submit those—they were in my portfolio. Preeti, you have gone too far this time!" With a grunt of frustration, he flung the magazine on her desk and started pacing the office, trying hard not to punch the wall. They were mostly glass, so that would not have ended well.

"While technically you didn't submit those for our use, they *are* here." Her calm tone only goaded him further. "I was actually doing both you and Melinda a favour, you know. I'm surprised you don't see it. And you were paid, as she will be for modelling when you give her this."

Preeti reached into her desk drawer and pulled out a white envelope with the *Fresh* logo and return address printed on the top left corner, but only "Melinda Myers" was written in Preeti's hand. She smiled and looked up.

"Are you going to sue me, Peter?" She held out the envelope.

Glaring, he snatched it from her, then yanked a pen from the organizer on her desk. On the back of the envelope, he scrawled Melinda's address.

"Give it to her yourself, and explain what you did—that I had nothing to do with it. She already doesn't want to talk to me. And here. You can have this back."

Peter reached into his shirt pocket and pulled out the folded cheque from *Fresh*, ripped it in half, and let the pieces fall in front of her. He snatched up his portfolio from the edge of her desk.

"I quit," he spat.

The glass door proved to be more resilient than he thought.

Preeti watched Peter storm out of her office, sighed, and tossed the discarded pieces of torn paper in the garbage bin. She picked up the envelope and regarded it thoughtfully. After a moment, she pulled out a fresh one, beginning to write the address information in its proper location on the blank face so it could be mailed. Then she stopped and pursed her lips, tapping the pen against them.

She had never seen Peter that upset with her in her life. Not even when they were teenagers and she had told Chanda Ravuraj that Peter had a huge crush on her and was going to ask her out (which might have been true, who knows? The crush part was not exaggerated, at any rate.) Word had gotten back to Chanda's father, who was outraged by "that forward Surati boy," as was their own father when Mr. Ravuraj came to discuss the matter with him. It had taken days to sort it all out, but after the dust settled, Peter cooled off and they were fine again. That was how their disputes usually went, but something told Preeti that things were different this time.

With a rare twinge of guilt, she tucked the unopened envelope with Melinda's address on the back into her purse. She would stop by the girl's apartment right after work and get this whole mess sorted out.

Then, without another thought, Preeti turned back to reviewing the story ideas for next issue's fashion pages.

CHAPTER EIGHT

Melinda stood up to survey her progress. She was in the middle of her living room floor—something she hadn't seen in over a year—with a pile of flattened dress boxes on one side, and scores of dresses laid in several piles on the couch on the other. She had been tempted to leave the couch bare, since it was such a novelty to be able to sit on it again, but she reminded herself that it would be available full-time once her task was complete.

Some of the dresses she had unboxed—the ones she loved the most and was the most proud of—were now hanging in her no-longer-barren closet. It felt strange to take ownership of the fact, but she *was* proud of her work. Each dress was a milestone passed, a design lesson learned, a vision transformed into reality. At the time she had made these gowns, she had simply been driven by the need to create, to keep busy … to forget. The end result was of little consequence, and received equally little thought after its single use on her "date night" with Robert. Until now.

After a quick jaunt to the kitchen to stretch her legs and grab a drink of water, she settled back down on the living room floor to finish sorting the last pile of boxes. She sorted the dresses into Sell, Keep, or Give Away piles, and the accompanying patterns were filed into a box for posterity. As she had figuratively moved backward through time in her fashion journey—like peeling up layers on an archaeological dig—the dresses had shifted from mostly going into the closet or the "Sell" pile to being almost exclusively put into the "Give Away" pile. She was glad for the lessons learned from those early dresses, but they paled in comparison to her more recent work.

Finally, Melinda reached the last box. She opened it and hesitated, then slowly pulled out the first dress she had ever made—the one she had meant to surprise Robert with on December 14, three years ago. It was a simple polyester crepe sheath dress in blush pink. She cringed a little as she examined the sloppy, uneven darts and the mismatched zipper. She had machine-stitched the hem, not wanting to take the time required for an invisible hand-done job, and the hem stitch wasn't even straight. Still … it was the only dress she had actually, truly intended to wear on a date with Robert.

On the day he died.

After a moment, she clambered to her feet, intending to hang the First Dress in her closet.

Just then, the intercom buzzed. "Melinda? Let me in. Please?"

Melinda hesitated in front of the speaker. Intense anger warred against a strong desire to see the man with the clipped Indian accent. Her hand came up to press the admittance button, then dropped while halfway to its destination. She stood there motionless, gripped with indecision.

Peter was about to buzz her again when another resident of the apartment building came out of the locked door and politely held it open for him. Smiling his thanks, he dashed through and leapt up the stairs, two at a time, to Melinda's second-floor apartment.

Melinda had just turned away from the intercom when she heard a man's tread echoing on the stairs, then the stairwell door crashing open, and then— while she stood frozen, hoping for and against the inevitable—a loud knock on her door.

"Melinda? Are you in there? Melinda? Please let me in. I really need to talk to you."

Melinda stared at the door and didn't move.

"Fine, I just need you to listen, anyway. First of all, I am so sorry about what happened with *Fresh*. I never

91

wanted to hurt you, and I hope you believe I had nothing to do with publishing those pictures."

Melinda's brow furrowed and her mouth twisted. He hadn't told them to publish the photos? Was he telling the truth? She felt a rhythmic swooshing in her ears, but she still didn't move.

Another tenant brushed past Peter on her way down the hallway. Peter leaned a hand against Melinda's door and waited until the woman was out of earshot before he continued.

"I—I know you've been lying to me about Robert. I found his obituary and an article about the crash online. I just don't know why you didn't tell me. And I don't know what I did to offend you, either. Well, until this magazine thing came up, anyway. Augh!"

Peter ran a hand over his mouth in frustration. He was doing this all wrong, but he didn't know how to do it any better. He was pretty sure that Melinda was listening to every word, since Sandra told him how Fred had taken Melinda home first thing that morning. But still, maybe she went out.

He reached into his messenger bag and grabbed a pen and the article he had printed out about the crash that killed Robert. He scribbled something across the back of the page, then slid it under the door to the apartment. With a final look at the door, he sighed and turned back toward the stairs.

As the silence stretched, Melinda took a hushed step forward to see if he'd gone. She was about to peek through the peephole when a printer page was shoved under the door. She held her breath and listened to Peter sigh in exasperation and leave before she bent to pick up the paper.

She remembered the article well. The exact same one was tucked into the side table in her room, snipped out of the newspaper when it was printed. Still, she scanned the words, surprised at how calmly she was able to read it now. Her eyes only moistened when she deciphered Peter's message to her.

Melly, I'm so sorry. Hurting you is the last thing I wanted to do. Please let me explain everything, and then you can hate me for the rest of your life if you want. Just let me try, because I really don't want you to hate me. Peter.

Wiping her eyes, she was surprised to find the rose-coloured dress still draped over her arm. She laid the page on the counter on top of the dusty wedding invitation, and then returned to the living room, where the sheath dress was the final article to land on the "Give" pile.

She gave it one last regretful look, but left it where it was and started packing the dresses into bags to take to their next destination.

"I'm sorry, Robert," she said to the smiling man in the engagement photo as she lifted the frame. "I may not be quite ready to move on. But I know that I have to let you go. It's time for me to start living again." As an afterthought, she also dug out the wedding invitation from under Peter's note.

She caught a glance of the handsome face in the photograph as she laid it in a shoebox with several others, and slipped the invitation down beside it. It was almost like Robert was smiling and nodding his approval. She smiled back, gently placed a thick envelope containing the engagement ring wrapped in tissue on top of the photo, and then slid the box under her bed.

"Pastor McKay?" Melinda said quietly, gently knocking on the open door of the man's office. The elderly gentleman with a fringe of white hair looked up from his cluttered desk, surprise flickering in his eyes.

"Melinda! Melinda Myers." A warm smile flooded his face as he stood up to greet her, clasping her hand in a firm grip. "Come in, come in!" He guided her to the padded chair facing his desk.

She thanked him and settled herself, dropping her purse onto the carpeted floor and unbuttoning her coat.

He slid back into his own chair and leaned forward. "To what do I owe the pleasure?"

Melinda was surprised at how glad she was to see him again. She had sat under his teaching most

Sundays during her childhood and teenage years. He was also the pastor who had buried her mother, her father, and who was supposed to marry her and Robert. Pastor Ralph McKay and his late wife, Edith, had spent many Sunday afternoons in the Myers' home. In fact, he was the closest thing she had to a grandfather that she could remember. However, after her father—and then Robert—had passed away, she had stopped attending church, shutting Pastor McKay and the rest of her church family out of her life.

Seeing him now, she resisted the urge to jump up and hug him.

"It's really good to see you, Pastor McKay," she said, a genuine but hesitant smile on her face. "I know it's been a long time." She twisted her fingers in a tight knot, then took a breath. "I came here today because I have a question that I am hoping you can answer."

"Well," he smiled, "I will do what I can. What's troubling you, child?"

After taking another deep breath, she dove in. "Can someone be … cursed?" She searched his face to see his reaction.

Pastor McKay sobered, put his elbows on his desk, clasping his hands under his chin as he regarded her thoughtfully. "What kind of a curse are you asking about?" he said at last.

"Well, could someone be cursed, say, to not be allowed to be close to anyone? Or that those close to them would be in danger … possibly mortal danger?"

It sounded kind of silly when she said it out loud—even to her own ears—but she desperately needed to know.

If it *was* possible, it would confirm her suspicions. She would become a hermit, move to the Northwest Territories and live off the land like the Inuit, so she wouldn't endanger anyone else ever again. But if it wasn't … she barely dared to breathe, waiting for his response.

He sat back. "I can think of several instances in the Old Testament where God cursed the families of someone who had rebelled against him, and they all died. In those cases, the family members themselves were also usually living in rebellion to God, so the punishment was just for all."

Melinda exhaled, her shoulders slumping and head drooping as she nodded slowly in resignation. The tender sprout of hope in her heart withered and died a cruel death in the dry, cracked soil of reality. "I thought so," she said, lifting her purse and standing up to go in one fluid motion.

"Wait, Melinda. Please." Pastor McKay held out his hand. "I'm not finished, child."

Melinda turned back toward him, but didn't sit down.

"Do you think you are under such a curse?" He met her eyes with a steady and concerned gaze.

With tight lips, she nodded.

"I see," he said, leaning back in his chair again. "And why would you think that?"

Melinda forced the words from a dry mouth. "Because I walked away from God," she said. "I was angry with him, and refused to serve him anymore."

"Hmm. So you believe that God cursed you for rejecting him." He nodded, his eyebrows drawing together. "Tell me, child, when did this unforgiveable act of rebellion against God occur?"

When she didn't respond, he prodded her. "Was it *your* rebellion that condemned Robert, the god-fearing man you loved, to death?" He raised his eyebrows. "Or your father, who served as a deacon in this very church and set an example of humility and charity to all who knew him?"

Melinda's shoulders still slumped, and she refused to meet his gaze.

"But you were only seven—or was it six?—years old when your mother died. Was it still in the tender years of your childhood that you turned your back on your maker, thus bringing down his wrath on you and all of those dear to you?"

As he exposed her fears for the lies they were, Melinda's tenuous emotional control was demolished. She fell back into the chair, covering her face with her hands, and sobbed from the depths of her soul.

Pastor McKay shuffled around the desk to sit in the chair next to her and placed a comforting hand on her shoulder.

"Melinda, I have known you from the moment your dear mother gave birth to you. I watched you grow up, and I was with you through your darkest hours. I know that it was only after you lost those most precious to you that you became angry with God and turned away." He squeezed her shoulder reassuringly. "It's okay—he is not upset by your anger, he understands. He has never stopped loving you. He's calling you back to him—you know that, don't you?"

Melinda nodded. She suddenly *knew* that the swirling whirlpool of loneliness in her spirit was not because she had lost Robert, or even her father or mother. Like a floundering swimmer with lungs on fire, she could finally see the surface where the Breath of Life waited. Hope beckoned within her. *Come back to the Father*, it said. *Come back to me.*

But she was not quite ready. Through her tears, she whimpered, "Then why did they die?"

Pastor Ralph sighed and patted her shoulder soothingly. "I can't tell you that for certain. The only one who can answer that question is the Father himself. But I know it was not out of malicious intent toward you, child. He loves you more than life, which is why his own son, Jesus, died on that cross so long ago—to redeem you, so that you can go live with him eventually. Your mother believed that, as did your father and Robert." He sighed. "Maybe God took them because it was simply time for them to come home."

Melinda's tears were quieter now, but she still sat with her face covered, sniffling. Pastor McKay handed her a box of tissue.

"Why don't you take some quiet time in the sanctuary and talk to your heavenly Father about this?" he said. "No one will bother you there. I will be right here if you need anything."

Melinda nodded, and then stood, taking her purse and the tissue with her.

Before she stepped out of the office, she paused. "Thank you, Pastor McKay."

He smiled gently. "Welcome home, Melinda."

The Friday Night Date Dress

CHAPTER NINE

Over a week later, Melinda crunched across the snow to her apartment building, head still reeling from the events of the afternoon as she fumbled in her purse for her keys.

She had taken a cab to the upscale commission clothing store downtown where she had dropped off about two dozen of the dresses from the "Sell" stash she accumulated the previous Tuesday. When she called the store that morning to see if any of the dresses had moved and to ask if they were ready for more, the lady on the other end of the phone laughed at her incredulously.

"Moved!" she almost barked in a tone that seemed at odds with her proper British accent. "Why didn't you tell me that you were the Melinda Myers on the cover of that hoity-toity ladies' magazine right now? After the first couple disappeared before I could say 'Sally's your aunt'—and both buyers amazed at the bargain prices for 'a Melinda Myers original'—we put up the price for the rest of them. You better get on down here, dearie, and bring the whole kit and caboodle, whatever you've got left."

When Melinda got to the store, there was a giant-sized enlargement of the current cover of *Fresh* in the window, and a hand-written sign in block letters made with Magic Marker that read "Now carrying Melinda Myers!" Her disbelief only increased when she got inside and the stately shopkeeper informed her that only one of the previous dresses remained. The stylish-but-matronly woman eagerly took the dresses Melinda had brought with her, expressing genuine admiration as each was hung on a clothes rack one-by-one to be steamed and displayed later.

"Ladies have been asking if we can get these in other sizes. Is that possible?"

Melinda shook her head in astonishment. "I, um, I don't know. Let me think about it."

After all the dresses had been hung, the stout woman reached behind the counter and pulled out an envelope with Melinda's name on the front. "Here are your earnings, dearie. Go ahead, take a look."

Melinda opened the unsealed flap and glanced at the figure on the cheque.

"How is this possible?" she asked, certain that all of the dresses together could not have sold for so much, let alone her commissions on the first couple of dozen generating such an amount. It was more than she made waitressing in almost two months.

"We ended up selling most of those dresses for over four hundred dollars each." Her voice took on a mothering tone. "Dearie, I'm glad you brought these to my store, but you really ought to consider going into business for yourself. You are a very talented designer."

Melinda was still mulling those words over as she reached the front door of her building.

"Melinda! Ms. Myers!" a woman's voice called from behind her. Looking around, she saw Preeti jogging awkwardly toward her in high-heeled leather boots from the curb where a cab sat. Melinda's eyes narrowed, but she held the door open and let the fashionably-dressed woman enter the warm foyer ahead of her.

"Thanks for waiting," Preeti smiled.

"I have nothing to say to you." Melinda glared, crossing her arms over her chest.

Preeti's smile faded. "I … guess I deserve that. Look, I just came to give you this. Sorry it took so long." She handed Melinda an envelope, her address scribbled in Peter's handwriting. "It's a cheque. And … I also want to say I'm sorry. I did not mean to cause problems for you. Believe it or not, it was because I believed in your talent—and Peter's—that I printed that article. I truly wanted to help you both. And you wouldn't believe the positive feedback we've been getting. People are raving about your work, Ms. Myers."

Melinda's arms remained crossed for a moment, and then she begrudgingly took the envelope. "*You* did it? Peter didn't tell you to print those photos?"

"No." She laughed sharply. "In fact, he was quite perturbed about the whole thing, threatened never to speak to me again, et cetera. You know, typical baby brother tantrum."

Despite the warmth that flooded her on hearing that Peter had been telling the truth, Melinda eyed the other woman coldly. "No, I don't, actually."

Preeti hesitated. "Of course not. Sorry. Well, I guess it's actually good that it took me a week to get over here, because now I also have this to give you." She handed over another envelope of high-quality linen paper. Melinda's eyes widened when she saw the logo of a well-known Toronto-based design company on the return address. "From what they told me on the phone, they would like to discuss bringing you on as another design partner."

Melinda took the envelope and nodded. "Anything else?"

"Yes there is, actually." Preeti hesitated, then hurried on in a rush. "Peter hasn't dated many girls, but the few he has have usually broken his heart. Still, I've never seen him so torn up as he has been for the last couple of weeks. I'm pretty sure the reason is you. I know you most likely have your reasons, and I don't mean to pry, but please … would you call him? Let him get some closure? I don't want to see him wrecked because of a girl he didn't even date. He is much too decent of a man for that."

Melinda didn't say anything, but nodded.

"Don't wait too long. His phone number is only good until Sunday."

"Why?"

"He took a photography job in Vancouver. He's moving."

Melinda's heart felt like it had stopped. She stared at Preeti with her mouth hanging open. *That's only two days away!*

Preeti put her leather-gloved hands in her pockets and shifted her feet. "Okay. Well, I guess I have taken up enough of your time. Goodbye, Ms. Myers." She left, taking careful steps on the icy sidewalk until she climbed back into the cab.

Climbing the single flight of stairs to her apartment, Melinda's head reeled as if she had been struck. She left the envelopes, forgotten, on top of the counter and sank onto the couch, stunned.

She knew two things for certain—Peter had loved her. And she finally realized it was safe to love him back.

But now, it might be too late.

On Saturday, December 14, Melinda awoke early, her stomach already balled into knots. After she had calmed down the previous evening, she had made two phone calls and then gotten to work. Even though she had been awake well into the wee hours of the morning, nerves and habit still woke her up at 6:00 a.m. But she had no intention of going to work today.

Her original plan for the day was to stay home, stay in bed, and hide from the world. She had taken the day off weeks ago with that exact intention, knowing that trying to work on the anniversary of Robert's death would have been completely impossible for her. But yesterday, her plans had changed.

She hastily dressed in the emerald-and-lemon bird-printed dress that had kept her up so late. It had been so long since she had worn anything but monochromatic tones or the gaudy blue waitressing uniform that she took a moment to admire the effect on her complexion. Her cheeks looked rosy, but she suspected that was also because of nerves.

An hour later, she was ready to go. It was much too early to leave, and she tried to calm down by reading and sipping tea. When she realized that she was re-reading the exact same page for the third time and still not comprehending a word, she gave up and closed the book. Looking at the clock, she decided that maybe it wasn't too early to go out now and called a cab.

At precisely 7:59 a.m., she buzzed Peter's apartment from the foyer of his building.

"Melinda?" a groggy-sounding Peter mumbled through the intercom. "You're very early for a Saturday."

When the door clicked and buzzed, Melinda rushed in.

Peter answered his door breathing hard. He was dressed in jeans and a white T-shirt, and Melinda noted with amusement that his socks were mismatched. Besides rumpled hair and a stubbly chin, he gave no other sign of being unprepared for her early arrival. He had been expecting her ... just maybe not before 10:00 a.m.

"Tea?" he asked as she struggled out of her boots.

"Yes, thank you," she said, her stomach clenching at the upcoming conversation. She took a deep, steadying breath as she hung up her coat.

While Peter fiddled around in the kitchen, Melinda settled onto his couch and smoothed the skirt of her dress, then looked around. The apartment was fairly tidy and tastefully decorated in muted, rich colours, accented with polished wood sculptures and art depicting the exotic flair of Peter's home country. Photography books graced the heavy, glass-topped wooden coffee table in front of her, and on the far wall she spotted a dark wooden bookshelf next to the TV. She tilted her head and saw John Grisham and Clive Cussler novels, books titled in a strange script that she thought must be Hindi, and a few engineering textbooks.

Peter set a heavy stoneware mug of Indian-style boiled chai tea in front of her on the elegantly-carved table, and then settled himself into an overstuffed leather chair on the other side.

"I didn't know you liked John Grisham." She picked up the steaming mug and blew across it.

He glanced at the bookshelf and shrugged.

"There are a lot of things you don't know about me," he said simply. He drew in a deep breath. "Listen, Melly—uh, Melinda, about those photos. I—"

She shook her head. "Preeti explained everything," she said. "I know it's not your fault."

His features were unreadable. "Oh," was all he said. The silence between them began to stretch uncomfortably.

Melinda fidgeted with her mug, then looked him in the eye. "Preeti also told me you are moving to Vancouver."

"Yep," Peter nodded once.

"I've been offered a position at a design house in Toronto," she said.

"Really? That's great. Really, really great."

When he didn't add anything, Melinda decided it was time to bite the bullet.

"Peter … I …" She sighed heavily. "I thought it was my fault. That Robert died, I mean."

Peter's eyes widened, then his brow furrowed. "Why would you think it was your fault?"

She rotated her cup between her hands. "This might sound strange, but I need to tell you all of it, so can you bear with me?"

He nodded, studying her.

She took another deep breath to slow her heart, then began.

"When I found out Robert was going on that five-day haul, I didn't want him to go. My dad had just died two weeks before, and I was terrified of being left alone so soon. We weren't living together, but Robert had been sleeping on my couch since Dad had passed, just to keep me company. But he had to go—he had to work, you know?"

She paused to take a sip of tea and collect her thoughts. "I thought I might go crazy if I just sat there and stared at the walls until he got back. Then I remembered that we had found my mom's sewing stuff when we had been putting Dad's things into storage. I went and found her machine, a pattern that I thought would fit me, some out-of-date fabric, and started making a dress."

Peter looked confused, but he just sipped his coffee and waited.

She took another sip of tea, then continued. "Robert always used to joke that the only reason he was marrying me was so he could finally see me in a dress. I was a real tomboy, you see. My dad had never minded, and neither had Robert, but I thought I would surprise him."

Her mouth twisted as she recalled that horrible night. "I got the dress done in time, but the night before Robert was supposed to come home, he called and told me that he was coming home a day later—the airline had rearranged his schedule. I pouted and fussed, not wanting him to stay away one moment longer than necessary. The next morning he texted that he was just getting on a plane—he had managed to catch a ride home on another pilot's flight. He would be home that night after all." She looked down. "Only, he wouldn't."

Her voice cracked. "I was getting ready to meet him when I found out that the plane had gone down." She clutched her mug with white-knuckled fingers, eyes moistening.

Peter leaned forward and gently tried to console her. "The article said that it was a mechanical failure. It was not your fault."

Melinda nodded. "I know. At least, I do now. But I have blamed myself for years that Robert was even on that flight. If I hadn't wanted to see him so badly and made such a fuss, he would have come home the next day and we would have been happily married five weeks later."

She had expected to break down in tears right then, and was surprised that she got through this confession without her heart being squeezed in the familiar vise-grips of guilt and shame. A surprising calm filled her spirit, and it was almost as though she felt the Father's presence envelop her in peace. *It wasn't your fault, my child*. She exhaled and closed her eyes in silent acknowledgement and gratitude.

"Was that when you began designing your dresses?" Peter asked in the silence that followed.

"Yes." She sighed. "I didn't want to see anyone, talk to anyone, or do anything for several weeks. Then one day I went and dug out my mother's entire fabric stash and started putting a dress together. When it was finished, I pretended that Robert and I were going on a date. I finally 'told' him everything that I had been needing to say to him and couldn't." She studied the creamy tea.

"It helped, a little. But … After Robert died, and Mom and Dad had already passed … Well, I … I was terrified that I must be cursed." She glanced up to see his reaction. His dark eyes showed only deep concern.

"I was afraid to let anyone else help me, in case they … uh … got hurt, too. So eventually, people stopped trying. I managed to close the door on everyone, but only two people refused to stop knocking. Robert's sister Nadia … and you."

She looked up at him again, straight into his eyes. Those bottomless black eyes were now burning into her soul, filled to the brim with compassion, and something else she couldn't—or daren't—name. She couldn't bear it, and her gaze fell onto her tea mug instead. She set it on the coffee table, then regained her resolve and looked up imploringly into his eyes, willing him to understand.

"I'm so sorry, Peter. I was only trying to protect you. Everyone who ever loved me has ended up … dead." She started shivering and wrapped her arms around herself to try to control the shaking. "I believed if I loved you, I would have to push you away."

With those words, the final lie in the dam she had been building for the last three years crumbled, and she started shaking with sobs. She cried for her father, and for Robert, and for all the scars she thought would never heal. As she cried, she felt the tears finally washing away all the pain she had held in for so long.

Peter's arms were already around her, enveloping her in heat and safety and security. He shushed her gently as she wept, holding her until her emotions were spent.

When she had finally stopped shaking and her tears subsided to the occasional sniffle, he pulled back a little to look in her eyes, cupping her chin in his hand. "Melly, I am so sorry for everything you have been through. But it's okay, now. You're here, I'm here, and I'm not going anywhere."

"Wha—what?" She dabbed at her face with a tissue. "What about Vancouver?"

"Silly girl," Peter said, smiling and stroking her hair.

Melinda smiled, too, at the way he said "gull."

"I was only going there because I couldn't bear to be here without you."

"You—you were?" She blinked.

"Mm-hmm. I'll even go to Toronto, if that's what you want. I'm sure I can find things to take pictures of there."

"You mean you don't want to put in for a transfer with UPS?" she said, hiccupping as she tried to make a joke.

He laughed, then brushed away the last few tears from her cheeks.

"I love you so much," he whispered. Then he gently pressed his lips against hers.

Electricity crackled into every extremity of Melinda's body, and tears started tracking her cheeks once more.

"What is the matter?" Peter pulled back in concern.

Melinda smiled through her tears. "I just never thought I would be this happy again."

"Cry when you're sad, cry when you're happy … I will never in all my life understand women," Peter teased.

Melinda laughed and hiccupped again, which made them both giggle even more.

"You don't have to understand them all," she teased shyly. "Just me."

He kissed her again, and his arms tightened around her.

"That's a challenge I will gladly take on," he murmured into her hair.

Melinda held him as tightly as she could, her head resting on his shoulder. She took a deep breath and felt her spirit breathe in the safety, security, and freedom of being loved. She wasn't alone anymore. And she wasn't cursed. And Peter loved her. She knew it was December outside the window. But in her soul, spring had arrived.

It was a long time before either of them relaxed their embrace to pull away.

"There is something else I need to do today," Melinda said at last, "and I was hoping you might agree to come with me."

"What is that, my love?" Peter kissed her cheek softly and stroked her hair as they snuggled on the couch. The events of the last hour seemed so surreal, he felt as though he were floating in the upper ionosphere somewhere.

"Robert's family is holding a private remembrance party this afternoon. I haven't seen any of them in over two years, and I really want to go. Once, they were my family, too." She hesitated. "Um, it would mean a lot if you would come with me. Would that be too weird for you?"

"Of course not. I would love to go! When do we need to leave? And where are we going?"

The Friday Night Date Dress

"They live in Brooks, a little town an hour or so east of here. If we catch a cab to the Greyhound station now, we should get there just in time."

"What, *now?*" Peter sat up, pulling his arm loose. "I'm hardly dressed for the occasion. And I haven't even eaten breakfast yet!"

Melinda giggled and held up her two thumbs and forefingers, crossed to make a rectangle with Peter in the middle of the frame. "Click! Gotcha!" she said, winking at him.

His face broke open in a wide grin and he laughed out loud. Melinda laughed, too, and he warmed at the sight of her looking so happy.

"It's good to hear you laugh." He gently laid his hand on her cheek. Then he stepped back and cocked his head. "That's a pretty dress. Did you make it?"

"Of course I did. I made it to surprise you." She gave a mincing curtsy. "And seriously, we need to leave in about an hour. I'll fix you some toast and eggs while you go change your socks."

He glanced down at his mismatched footwear and laughed again. "Sounds good," he said, already heading toward the bedroom. "But I think we'll take my car, if that's okay with you."

"A vehicle. Right. Why don't we take your car?"

Peter chuckled as he left the room. He could hear the cupboard doors rattling in the kitchen as he hunted down some matching socks.

Maybe they didn't even need the car. He was pretty sure that this morning he could fly.

CHAPTER TEN

"… And now, by the power vested in me, I pronounce you husband and wife," Pastor McKay announced, his voice booming over the grassy lawn from the loudspeakers set up near the gazebo. Melinda's stomach fluttered, her eyes locked onto Peter's. He was already leaning toward Melinda with an eager grin as the pastor added, "You may kiss your bride."

Peter and Melinda broke apart to cheers from the gathered crowd.

Pastor McKay raised his voice to be heard over the applause and imbued his next declaration with dramatic excitement. "It is my privilege to introduce … Mr. and Mrs. Peter and Melinda Surati!"

As the guests stood and clapped even louder, he stepped away from the mic to shake hands with the bride and groom. "God bless you both," he said, grinning with delight.

Melinda leaned close to the old man's ear. "Thank you, Pastor McKay." Then she flung her arms around him and kissed his cheek. He chuckled and squeezed her affectionately in return.

Melinda turned and took Peter's hand, and they gazed at each other for a moment before they faced their cheering guests from the top step of the gazebo. The opening riff of a Hindi love song whose title meant "beloved" started playing over the loudspeakers.

"Shall we, *maahi ve*?" grinned Peter, echoing the song.

Melinda giggled and nodded. She and Peter bounced down the stairs, Nadia and Preeti each joining arms with their husbands and falling into place behind the bridal couple as they proceeded down the cobblestones.

Melinda glanced back at the glowing Indian woman who followed behind her and Peter in the wedding procession, and smiled when their eyes met. Preeti smiled back, then glanced down to steady herself as her heels caught on the edge of a cobblestone—her baby bump was quite pronounced now, and she was still getting used to the difference in her centre of gravity. Preeti's husband Michael steadied her with a hand on her back.

Melinda couldn't believe how well the day had worked out. She and Peter had wanted the wedding to be simple, and since Peter's family was also Christian, being married by Pastor McKay was the natural choice.

While the wedding was mostly Western in tradition, they had managed to incorporate some Eastern flair. Red and gold embroidery accented Melinda's flowing white damask silk gown (which she had designed herself, of course). The trim matched the gold embroidery on the jacket hem and sleeves of Peter's Asian-cut white suit. Both the bride and groom wore a garland of red flowers around their necks, the heady aroma moving with them like a cloud of perfume.

Despite the Indian tradition of inviting nearly everyone the couple—and the parents of the couple—knew to a wedding, they had managed to convince Peter's parents that a small gathering was what they wanted. Melinda was thankful for more reasons than just financial ones—the minimal stress of the wedding preparations had allowed her to spend some time getting to know her new in-laws better since their arrival from Mumbai several days before. As it was, many more of Peter's relatives than she had expected to make the trip were among the guests.

Of course, not much of the wedding stress had been hers to deal with, anyway. Preeti had Bonnie, her mercenary assistant, plan the wedding. The woman made efficiency into an art form—she had made sure the whole event ran like a well-oiled machine. Melinda could see Bonnie now, standing behind the last row of chairs, continually scanning to make sure everything was proceeding exactly as it should.

Melinda mused about how much had changed in her life in the six months of her and Peter's whirlwind courtship and engagement. Not least surprising was that she and Preeti had become fast friends.

It had begun after Melinda had gone to Preeti for advice on how to go about establishing herself as an independent designer in the Canadian market. That initial meeting led to the surprising realization that they actually had a great deal in common. Before long, shopping and tea dates together were regular entries on their schedules.

As the wedding party entered a huge white tent and lined up to greet their guests in a traditional receiving line, Nadia wrapped Melinda in a huge hug, tears of joy running down her face. "I know we aren't technically sisters, but I'm as proud of you as if we were. And so very happy. Peter is one of the good ones. Congratulations."

Melinda returned the hug gratefully. "Thank you for always being my friend and never giving up on me, Nadia," she said, tears filling her eyes as well. With a smile, they stepped into their places as the first guests arrived to shake their hands and wish them well.

"Well, Peter, you managed to get a weekend off, did you?" Edwin Clarkson teased as he shook the groom's hand.

Reuniting with Robert's family had been one of the biggest blessings to Melinda—they had re-adopted her as their own daughter, and had tested and accepted Peter with all the good-natured teasing of incorporating an extra son into the family. Edwin had even given Melinda away.

"Yes, well, I figured it might be a bit awkward to be the photographer at my own wedding," Peter jested back, clasping hands and exchanging gruff hugs with the tall, thin man. Peter had been able to walk away from his delivery job several months before, filling most Saturdays with capturing other people's wedding memories. He also worked nearly full-time with *Fresh* and was expanding his home studio clientele.

Melinda glanced proudly at her new husband—*my husband!*—then hugged Edwin and his wife, Valerie.

"You look stunning, my dear." Valerie's eyes twinkled under greying brown hair. "And you, young man," she said, taking on a mock scolding tone as she turned back to address Peter. "Take good care of this girl, or you shall have *me* to answer to."

"Well, I wouldn't want to risk that," Peter grinned. "Don't worry, Mrs. C., I will have her barefoot and pregnant in no time."

A step behind Valerie, Peter's mother's mouth fell open in shock at the comment. Preeti leaned over and smiled at her mother reassuringly.

"Don't worry, Mama. Peter is only joking—I think he has been spending a little too much time around these redneck Albertans." She fixed her brother with an intense glare. "You were only teasing, right, Peter?"

"Of course I was," he laughed, hands raised in mock defense. "What kind of unsophisticated swine do you take me for?"

Mavis Surati looked only slightly mollified, and rattled off something in Hindi that made Peter put on a chastened look. Preeti and her father laughed out loud.

"Yes, Mama. I will." Peter squeezed the short, plump Indian woman in the glittering sari tightly before extending his hand to his father.

Melinda caught Peter's eye with a questioning glance, but he just gave a subtle shake of his head and grinned sheepishly.

"Melinda," said Mavis with a wide smile, holding her new daughter-in-law's arms in ring-bedecked hands. "I am so glad to welcome you to our family. I can't wait to get to know you better, but from what I have seen so far, I know Peter couldn't have made a better choice."

"Thank you, Mama," smiled Melinda as Mavis swooped in for a hug that completely flattened her bridal garland.

As the procession continued, Melinda floated in a tangerine haze. To have gone from diner waitress to up-and-coming designer—with her own online store, a couple of professional seamstresses assembling her designs, and preparations for her first New York Fashion Week show underway—was nothing short of amazing.

But to have gone from such utter aloneness to having not one, but *two* families to call her own in so short a time—several friends among them—was enough to make her tremble with joy.

While she didn't expect the rest of her life to be painless and trouble-free, she basked in this moment of complete contentment, soaking in every drop. She had a calm assurance that she would never again be alone. God had made her this promise before she was even born, but it was only in that quiet sanctuary at Pastor McKay's church last December that she had finally answered His call—*I am with you always. I will never leave you, nor forsake you. Come back to me, my daughter.* Her heart, once a shattered mirror, had been restored into a glorious glass window that displayed the story of her Father's love through every lovely pane.

She felt Peter's hand settle momentarily on the small of her back and shot him an adoring smile in a brief moment between well-wishers.

Suddenly, she thought she caught a familiar face out of the corner of her eye, and turned back toward the line in surprise. Standing just beyond the queue of slowly-moving guests, across the lawn toward the gazebo, she thought she saw her father grinning widely, his blue eyes glinting. One of his arms was around her mother, young and radiant in her favourite plum-coloured dress, and the other was around Robert, smiling and blowing a kiss at her in his captain's uniform. Tears of joy filled her eyes as she smiled and nodded back, and then the image was gone.

No, she didn't know what adventures the next chapter of her life would bring—but for the first time in years, she was eager to find out.

About the Author

Talena Winters loves tea, travel, music, whole food, sewing, knitting, reading, and chocolate. Besides fiction, she also writes a blog, knitting patterns, and musical theatre (among other genres of music). She currently resides on an acreage in the Peace Country of northern Alberta, Canada, with her husband, four boys, a Golden Retriever named Sunshine, and an assortment of farm cats and chickens.

Talena would love to be a mermaid when she grows up.

You can find her on the web at www.talenawinters.com, Twitter @TalenaWinters, and Facebook at www.facebook.com/talenawinters.artist.

Dear Reader,

Thank you for purchasing this book. I hope you enjoyed it. If so, I would really appreciate it if you would leave a review on the platform you purchased this from to spread the word.

Since writing is how I help feed my family, it would mean *so* much if you would drop by your favourite book seller and purchase a copy for a friend or two.

I love to hear from you! Please stop by my website (www.talenawinters.com) and drop me a note, or email me at talena@wintersdayin.ca.

Yours,

Talena Winters

CPSIA information can be obtained
at www.ICGtesting.com
Printed in the USA
LVOW04s1737170716

496596LV00002B/3/P